ABBY'S
QUEST

Best wishes!

ABBY'S QUEST

JOANN BUIE

Independently published by Desert Wind Press LLC
www.desertwindpress.com

ISBN 978-1-956271-11-9 (paperback)
ISBN 978-1-956271-12-6 (ebook)

To my husband, Bo,
who encouraged me to write my stories,
believed in me,
who is my rock and my everything.

$\mathcal{P}$ROLOGUE

I knew the moment I threw my mortarboard cap into the air at my graduation from high school, that I would be totally on my own. No one would be there to support me, my hopes, and dreams any longer, not that I actually had anyone who cared to begin with, because I didn't. I will probably never see the few friends I made during my years there ever again.

It was bitter sweet for me, as I walked through the halls for my last time. I had my diploma in my hands, and had no after thought about leaving this town, or my life behind.

I wasn't leaving much to begin with. I lived from foster home after foster home since I could remember. I never gave the people any trouble, but most people only wanted to foster the little kids, and I was past that period of time. My latest foster home was with a spinster, that was so strict I didn't dare breathe without her permission.

All I knew about my parents was zilch, nada, nothing. I had been left at a designated safe place at a fire station at birth. Nothing else, but a bottle, and a few diapers knowing someone would provide the rest of what I would need.

It was hard being moved around so much at the beginning. Often I would hear my new family talking about me, saying how sad it was that I would grow up not knowing anything about my parents. I was about ten or eleven years old when I came to grips with reality, and decided to buckle down making the best of my situation to get myself out of this town, and away from all the reminders of not being wanted.

Once I turned sixteen, I was able to get a part time job to make a few extra dollars. I planned to save it all for my future, whatever that might hold. I was always looking in the newspapers for jobs in other areas that I would be qualified for. I was turned down by many of the jobs I applied for, mainly because of my age, and inexperience. Some people never even responded, which was a flat out no in my book.

Until the day I received a positive reply, I was beginning to lose hope, almost giving up. That day turned me around, when I accepted the position as a house sitter for a family being transferred overseas, and needing a house sitter.

The pay wasn't the greatest, but I had a small cottage on the property all to myself that was furnished, and I had to only clean the partially empty main house weekly. It was a beautiful Victorian home. I had the use of their washer and dryer in the basement. It seemed perfect for me, and I was excited. I had a job and would be moving out of state.

I didn't share my news with anyone, and really didn't think anyone would be happy for me if I had. I wasn't much of a social butterfly as I got older because of my school studies, and part time job keeping me busy. I knew my foster mother wouldn't have allowed any friends to visit me at the house, and heaven forbid I would even have a date. So, I was missing out on a lot of activities growing up.

My one ugly brown suitcase was packed, with all my worldly possessions by the morning of graduation, because I wouldn't be allowed back in the house once I received my diploma. My foster mother was glad to have the house back to herself, and made no bones on telling me just that. I had to drag that suitcase to school with me where I donned into my cap and gown, preparing for the walk across the platform to receive my diploma. I couldn't wait for that magical moment I have worked so hard to get.

My bus ticket was paid for by my new employers, and I would be on a Greyhound making my way to Jasper, Tennessee, by noon the very same day. I was looking forward to my new life, and adventure on my own. I took a seat by the window, and watched as the bus pulled away from the station. Before I knew it, I was out of the town I called home…a temporary home at that.

CHAPTER 1

As I packed my brown worn out suitcase, the night before my graduation from high school, I looked around my room wondering what my life would have been like, if I had known my birth parents, and we had been a family. I was going to be totally on my own after tomorrow, which I was excited about, yet terrified at the same time. I didn't know what was ahead of me, and what to expect around the next corner, but I knew I had to deal with whatever it was, because I had nothing else in life.

It had always been that way growing up. I had no one interested in my life, other than my caseworker that came around maybe once every six weeks, if I was lucky, to check on me, and my living arrangements. Most of the time she came in, and was back out within twenty minutes. Just enough time to ask how I am, how things were going, about my grades in school, and how my foster parents were with me. The questions never changed, and yet, I did okay, I thought. I wasn't a trouble maker, and my grades were high only because I worked hard at them. I had no one helping me at home with homework, or projects. It was all left up to me.

I had been working for the past two and a half years at a grocery store cashiering, and stocking, part time to save for this final day. My current foster mother made sure I knew that her obligation caring for me would end tomorrow, and had no sad feelings of seeing me leave her house. Clara was a lonely old spinster that was way too strict for me to have any feelings, but gratitude for her allowing me to stay through my high school years. I tried to make things easy for her, by helping her out with things around the house, never giving her any problems, but it was only in vain. She had the attitude children should not be seen, or heard, which allowed me to hole up in my room, as long as I wanted. I knew it could have been better at another foster home, but I was never able to change families.

I didn't have much to pack, but I was packing everything that belonged to me, for my new life, and adventure, in Jasper, Tennessee at a house sitting job that I accepted when offered it to me, through the internet. A middle aged professional couple going overseas on business dealings for the next two years, or more, that wanted to keep their house occupied somewhat. They were what I referred as **TINKS**. **T**wo **I**ncomes, **N**o **K**ids.

I had been turned down by so many people on my job searches, and I searched all the time sending resumes out daily. My boss at the grocery store wrote a beautiful letter on my behalf, but it wasn't enough with all the rejections I received back. Mostly stating because of my age, and non-experience, as the key factor in not hiring me. Jack didn't want me to leave my position at the grocery store, but understood my need to escape the town, and start a new life for myself away.

I don't think I was actually running away from my life, but I felt I needed to get away to get a new start. A place where no one knew me, or about me, like they did in this town. I looked up articles on the internet seeing if I could find a clue to who my parents were. There weren't any clues to be found, but several articles on the "baby abandoned at the fire station", and asking if anyone knew who I could belong to, to please step forward. No one ever inquired about me, so I lived in the foster care program my entire life.

I carefully hung my cap and gown over the door top for tomorrow morning on a wire coat hanger, and set my clothes out, before I went to get my shower. Afterwards, I packed my shampoo, and other toiletries I wouldn't need in the morning. I knew Clara wouldn't be coming to see me graduate, but I was okay with that. I wasn't expecting her to come, but it would have been nice.

As I laid down to fall asleep all the questions, and different scenarios, wandered into my mind that kept me awake longer than I wanted. I did fall asleep for a few hours, but once my alarm clock went off, I was ready to hit the road. I quickly, and quietly, dressed. All my belongings were packed in my suitcase, and a backpack, as I headed downstairs. I knew Clara was already awake, but not coming out to see me off. I spoke to her through her bedroom door thanking her for taking me in, and hope she has a wonderful day. No response from Clara at all, and I turned walking out the door for the last time. Guess it really hit me that Clara was serious, about being glad her obligation to care for me, was finally over. I sighed, and made my way out of her house walking the sidewalk for the last time, towards my school.

Hauling that suitcase to the school was embarrassing, and disheartening at the same time. I made sure not to look up as I made my way to my locker, so I wouldn't have to meet anyone staring at me, or hear the whispers. I had to put it in my locker sideways in order for me to close the door. No one mentioned it to me, but I knew that they knew why I had that suitcase with me. That was a good thing, because I was really feeling unwanted at this point. I wasn't sure if I would break down, and cry, or let my anger out on them. I didn't want to do either, so I just kept my eyes down trudging onward.

As we dressed into our cap and gown, I dug out the new white heels I bought special for that day. I wanted to fit in with all the others as much as possible, knowing full well, I never did fit in with anyone. It was important to me to buy those shoes as a statement, that I too could look like a graduate as well as them, and be proud of myself as well.

As we walked to the auditorium and on stage to receive our diplomas, I saw Jack with a few cashiers from work, sitting in the front row cheering for me. My heart melted knowing I had someone there making it special for me. I smiled at them, to let them know how happy that made me. Actually, I was almost in tears, but I would never let anyone see me cry.

After it was announced we were officially graduates of the school, we threw our caps into the air cheering as loud as the people that where there to see their graduate. I grabbed my cap off the ground to keep. Looking around, everyone was taking pictures of family, and with friends. Everyone seemed so happy, and friendly towards each other. I was headed out the door when Jack, and the cashiers caught up to me. They were happy for me, and gave me a gift to remember them by. It was a CD player with ear buds, and an assortment of CDs of music I enjoyed. I was happy about that, and that there was someone there for me. I hoped others saw that I too, had someone to congratulate me as well.

I thanked them giving them a hug, and as they left, I turned to retrieve my suitcase from my locker, to head for the bus station in town. It was a bittersweet feeling, as I walked down the quiet hallway of the high school with my shoes making the only hollow echo sound on the floor. Making for the door, I knew I would probably never walk that hallway again, or step inside the school. I didn't feel emotional one way, or the other. Guess it was like my life had been, nothing to get excited about.

I had stuffed my cap and gown into the side pocket of my backpack, put my gift from Jack, and the other cashiers, into my backpack I would carry with me. Once I was on my bus heading out of town, I looked out the window silently saying goodbye to everything there. The only place I had ever known. After about an hour of the trip, we had another stop to make, and more passengers boarded. A kind lady sat next to me. We chatted for awhile, until I excused myself to lean my head back, and fell asleep using my backpack for a pillow.

I slept for hours, until the bus came to a stop. The driver announced we would have an hour layover, and new driver. We were allowed to exit the bus to grab something to eat, and I grabbed my backpack to head out. I was so hungry, I could have eaten a cow right then. I ordered two mouth watering deluxe cheese burgers, fries and jumbo iced tea. While waiting for my order, I stocked up on other snacks, not knowing when we would be stopping again, that could hold me over until my next meal.

Once I ate my lunch, I was back on the bus, and we were shortly back on the road. I wouldn't arrive at my destination for another day, so I pulled a novel out of my backpack to read, until it was too dark out, and the overhead light too dim to see the words, without straining my eyes. I puffed up my make shift pillow against the window closing my eyes again for more sleep.

It was bright, and sunny outside, when I woke up. The sun was beating on my face through the window, and I could hear conversations starting up, from other passengers. I grabbed a juice box, and a granola bar, from my backpack to eat for my breakfast. I was glad I had bought the extra snacks when I did, because I was hungry more than I thought. I looked around the bus. Most people were sitting alone, so I didn't feel like I sent out bad vibes where no one wanted to sit with me. I was happier to be by myself actually. The scenery outside my window was green lush rolling hills, but nothing spectacular to look at, so I went back to reading my book.

My book was very interesting from a well known author, Aaron Malone, but as far as I was concerned, he was a nobody like me. I might add that this author knew how to place his words to bring his story to life. I had read a few other novels by him, and they were all interesting romance novels that had happy endings. I liked the happy endings, it gave me hope that maybe some day I would have a happy ending to my life.

We stopped at noon for another hour break, and again I bought a hot lunch as before knowing I had at least one hot meal a day in me. Only a few more hours until I reached my destination, and begin my new job. I was looking forward to that.

My new employers, Jonathan and Amber, said the bus stop was about a block from the house, and they would leave all the information needed in a large manila envelope inside the cottage, on the table. They had sent me the key to the cottage I would be living in when they hired me, and I hung on to it with my life.

Once my stop was announced, later that evening, I put my book inside my backpack ready to make my departure. I was the only one getting off there, and the driver mumbled about me wasting his time trying to locate my suitcase. Well, I'm not who put it under the bus, so he needed to just do his job to retrieve it for me. I was being very patient with him, and he could be a little bit kinder. He had a colorful selection of foul words he spat towards me. Once the driver removed my suitcase from cargo below the bus, he hurriedly got back behind the wheel, before I was less than a dozen steps away, putting his foot on the gas.

I looked around wondering where to go next. I was new to this area feeling very alone, and lost at the moment. It looked like a nice area of town, with big beautiful homes all around, huge trees lining the streets providing shade, and flowering baskets hanging from the lampposts. Gave it that warm fuzzy welcoming feeling I yearned for.

I spotted a plaza full of various stores that I made my way towards hoping I could get the information I need to find the street, and house. At the first shop, a very kind lady came out of the office to assist me. She introduced herself, as Molly, and I was in luck, the street was right smack in front of her shop. She also knew the house I spoke of.

I thanked her, and headed towards the house I would be house sitting. It was a block north of the main street going up a small hill. A beautiful house sat on the left that had a pasture, with beautiful horses grazing, before reaching it. There was a stone wall along the pasture half way up, then wire fencing the rest of the way. One horse walked along the side of the wall, as I walked toward, the house which I dubbed him Chestnut Charlie because of his coloring. I had an apple in my backpack from the bus trip that I quickly fed to him, and he bobbed his head in appreciation, as he chomped down on it.

I continued walking until I reached the house. It was a magnificent Victorian home, with a wrap around front porch, and huge windows with the upper portion made with stain glass. I walked up the driveway, under a veranda covered with English Ivy, that led to the white picket fence. The opened a gate to the backyard before noticing the cottage that would be home for me, for the next two years, or more. The yard was spectacular with lush green grass, a swing for couples under the large tree, and flowers in every spot designated for them. The cottage was quaint with the owner's garage attached to the front of the cottage as well.

I quickly unlocked the door stepping inside to take in what was to be my home. There wasn't much to see, but plenty of furniture, and a color TV to watch, as I scanned the room. Upon further inspection, the bedroom was to my left, with a bathroom attached. My bed was made, ready for me to fall into, and towels in the bathroom for me as well. I knew I was going to like it here already, and knew I made the right decision to take this job.

The kitchen was a combo kitchen, dining area and living room. My refrigerator was stocked with a few items to last me until I could get to the store myself. These people were so kind to think of all this.

Their letter to greet me, in the manila envelope, was packed full of information I might need, with a list of the people, and phone numbers that they use for the yard work, plumbing, etc. They told me to arrange the furniture any way I want in the cottage. It was my place to make it my home, and for me to be comfortable in. I smiled from ear to ear with everything happening to me now, and I thanked my lucky stars to be here. I let out a squeal of happiness smiling from ear to ear.

Amber also clued me in on the elderly lady living in the house next door. Her name was Miss Nelson, and she was a cantankerous old biddy, that was far from being friendly, but always peeking her head through the curtains to snoop thinking she might miss out on something. Heavens only know what was going through her mind, what she was up to, but as long as I kept my distance, I would be fine. That gave me a chuckle thinking another Clara, all the way down here. It didn't take me too long to get my things, and myself, settled in. Let's face it, I didn't have much with me. I moved a few things around to suit my style. Deciding I better run to the grocery store to get a few things that I wanted, and be back before it was too dark out. Being new to the area, I wasn't sure what to expect, but I didn't want to take chances either.

While I was shopping in the grocery store, Molly came up to me mentioning I must have found the house okay, and we chatted for a few minutes. She was the owner of the grocery store, as well as the small boutique next door. It wasn't long before we became good friends, but on a friendship that wasn't over bearing.

A few weeks later I decided to see what was what in her boutique. I had so much time on my hands after my house sitting chores were done, I was restless, needing to get out for awhile to window shop. It was always a great way to pass time. I was amazed with her selection of various items. I noticed many items featured Aaron Malone. That intrigued me as to why she had such a vast amount of items about, and on him, as well as the novels lining several shelves on the wall.

It didn't take me long to find out either. The huge mansion across the street was where he lived. There were many women of all ages that tried to see him, and have him autograph their book, or themselves. Molly explained it was a hoot watching the women drool when he was in the store. I think Molly had every book he wrote in her boutique, along with other various items that she had to restock nightly. She informed me they were really great friends as well, and he often came by to chat with her.

Molly asked what I was doing to occupy my spare time. I told her I was going absolutely stir crazy not having anything to do. She asked if I would be interested in working for her, at the boutique. One of her girls decided to leave, and she needed to fill her position in two weeks. I thought it over, knowing in my head I was going to take it, but didn't want to sound too eager, before telling her I would. I would be able to do the main house, and my little cottage cleaning, when I was off on the weekends. I was pretty pleased to think I would have two incomes coming in, and my life was starting to move forward. It was a great feeling, and I was feeling pretty positive about everything. Especially about my move here to Jasper.

I put the few groceries away that I bought when I got home, while listening to the radio, before I showered, making my way to bed exhausted, but content at the same time. I was going to make it on my own, I just knew I would do great given the right time, and place. I think I found it too, right here in Jasper, Tennessee.

CHAPTER 2

I woke refreshed and ready to tackle anything that came my way the following morning. When I was stretching my arms, I felt like I was on cloud nine. Things were finally looking up for me, and I was grateful. Grateful for everything I had at the moment. I was even grateful to Clara who allowed me to stay with her to finish my school years, as much as I know she didn't want me there most of the time.

I quickly got dressed, made and poured a cup of coffee, and toasted a bagel to go sit under the huge tree in the backyard, on the swing. Many times I would take my CD player with me, and listen to the music as well. Might be the place where I could release my feelings, thoughts, peaceful times, and not drag anything negative into my little home.

My little home. As small as it was, I absolutely loved it, and I was really feeling like I belonged there. Just the perfect size for one person, and I was glad to be the one occupying it for the next two years or more.

I had a strange feeling I was being watched several times while outside, and once I quickly glanced to the house next door to see that old biddy, Miss Nelson, had been watching me. As soon as she saw me look at her, she backed away from her window. I just wave smiling. For what good that would do, I wasn't sure, but I was going to try being friendly to her. Who knows why she is the way she is. There might be a reason, and I'm not the one to judge her.

Miss Nelson had a mammoth old maple tree in her backyard that hung several huge branches over my cottage. It kept my place shaded during the day in the hot summer months, but I was worried about it during the storms, and winter already. Maybe that was why Jonathon and Amber were at odds with her. It could be a potential danger under harsh conditions, if a branch would break falling on the cottage or garage.

I found an old bike in the storage unit beside the garage with a basket on the front, that I could get around on when the weather was good, which was most of the time as it seemed. Needed new tires, so I bought some replacing the old ones. A bike tire pump was in the storage unit I found, while doing a quick search. I quickly got the air in the tires. Soon I was able to ride it where ever I needed to go. It gave me some freedom to explore the neighborhood more. Saved my legs from all that walking, and still get the exercise needed. A win-win situation for me.

I was finally set in a routine that I could adjust, when needed. Before I knew it, I was starting my new job at the boutique. Couldn't sleep the night before as I should have, but I was excited. I arrived several minutes early to get the jest of things and a copy of the rules and regulations, from Molly. We sat in her back office before opening the store drinking a cup of coffee together, and getting to know each other better. She had paperwork for me to read, and sign as well. Everything sounded easy enough, and I felt things would run smoothly.

Molly's twin sister, Mary, worked across the street in that huge mansion, as Molly was telling me about Aaron Malone's family. Probably more than what I needed to know, but it was great to get some inside scoop on someone as famous as he was. Usually, I have to read the gossip in the tabloids, but I was getting my source right there in Molly's office. Everything she told me about the man intrigued me greatly.

Apparently, he had gone through a nasty divorce several years ago, and was sharing custody of their little girl, Carrie Ann, with his ex-wife. Aaron sounded like a wonderful father, but had bad taste in most women, in my opinion. Writing took up the majority of his time, but he had plenty of people working for him in the house and land. People were always over to visit daily making Carrie Ann living in a grown-up world, without knowing a childhood like most kids her age. That I thought was rather sad, but she seemed to do well with everything the way it is. The ex-wife, Diana, was there often to see that things were being done properly for Carrie Ann, calling the staff together to make her voice heard. She was more of a pain in the neck than anything, but Aaron bowed down to her still for some reason no one seemed to understand why.

My first day at the boutique flew by, and I was amazed at how many purchases were made. It never looked that busy when I went by the place, but I tell you, it was. I was done at five, and a few other people came in for the night shift, which was just part time until closing hours for restocking the items for about two hours.

I couldn't wait to get home, and relax on my swing with a tall glass of iced tea. I noticed I have spent more time on that swing when I was in need to think things through, or when I needed to just relax.

Molly had asked if I would be willing to fill in for the night shift, if needed once in awhile, which I agreed. Once I got home my feet were killing me, and I was exhausted. Maybe I agreed too soon with the way my feet were hurting. After about an hour I grabbed a quick bit to eat, soaked in the tub, and hit the sack as soon as I could. I don't think my head hit the pillow before I was asleep either.

After my first week there, I started getting into the groove of things easily, and I was able to adjust my sleeping hours so I could get a movie watched on the TV, or of the many DVDs that were in the house's family room cabinet. I had a set pattern on doing things now. Some nights I would just sit on the swing to relax, and other than that, I didn't do much else.

One of the other girls working in the boutique, Debbie, was going to college part time. She gave me many brochures to read on her college, and after awhile I thought it might be good to take a few classes each semester. What I really needed was the money to take the classes. They were more than what I could budget in my life at this time. Maybe in the fall I could revisit that idea. For right now, I was enjoying my life at peace, with everything going on while earning more money than I ever thought possible.

Debbie and I were becoming pretty close friends. She had an apartment not far from work, but we never socialized after work. That was okay by me. Besides, she had a boyfriend she was pretty involved with. I know the old saying, "two's company, three's a crowd," so why put myself in that situation? I am content at what I do, and where I am. Another thing, I didn't want to talk about my life to anyone either. I didn't feel the need to share any of that with anyone else.

Many times while at work, I saw Aaron Malone go into Molly's office. I could hear them chatting, but never could hear anything more than noise. An occasional outburst of laughter, so I knew they were just having a great time visiting. He would always give her a hug, and kiss her cheek, before leaving. It looked to me like they were not just friends, but very good friends. He was so many years younger than Molly, but who knows, not my problem.

Whenever Aaron came in, the place was super busy with every female known to mankind just hoping get a glimpse of him, and maybe get him to autograph his newest book. It never failed. Molly never minded them there, because it increased her sales of the items she had concerning him. Believe you me, Molly had everything a person could think of having on Aaron Malone!! It was like she was the one who had to have it all herself. He never stayed long after his visit with Molly, always in a hurry to escape the rush of the crowd.

I would think he would enjoy the crowds, but he didn't seem to want to linger very long. I did notice that his eyes seemed to have a sad look in them. Molly had said he was taken for a lot of money from his ex-wife, and maybe that had something to do with it. No one needs to be taken advantage of in my book, but I wasn't one to do anything about that. I just kept my distance working in the store whenever he was around.

Molly would stand in her office doorway smiling. Don't know if it was from their visit, or her knowing the sales of his stuff would make a good day for her. Who knows, maybe she had him coming over often, so it would boost her sales, and I couldn't blame her there!

It didn't hurt that his romance novels were hot and steamy either, and from his looks, I bet every one of those women dreamed they were the ones he was writing about. Maybe in their dreams they had hoped he would ask one of them to join him, but he always left the place by himself.

He was very mystic, and when he spoke there was so much kindness in his voice that made the women drool on every word he spoke. Didn't hurt that he was very good looking either. You could smell his cologne linger hours after he left. One could get caught up in their fantasies over him easily. He had impeccable taste in his cologne, and his clothes as they were very nice. I had to admit that myself.

It always made for an interesting day when he came in with the chatter from the other women. I could gaze at him from a distance, and no one saw anything on my part. His dark hair was so thick with soft curls knowing that whoever he went to for his haircuts knew exactly how to cut it perfect. His dimple on the left side of his face would appear every now, and then when he did smile, which didn't seem to be too often.

However, his kindness wasn't something to be overlooked. Whatever hurt him as bad as it was, he knew when to put the charm on for the women. I noticed he always had a felt pen on him, just incase he was asked to autograph a book, which was quite often. Must be something every author did.

I was able to see Molly standing by her office door smiling from ear to ear with everything going on with Mr. Malone, and her customers, without her catching me watching her. She was pleased with the sales, and seeing Mr. Malone mingle with the women which was something I quickly learned that happened often in her boutique. Was it planned or random visits by Mr. Malone, I wasn't sure, but there was no set time or day that he would show up to visit. Molly always had time to speak with him too. She would stop whatever she was doing to visit, and the door always remained shut during those visits.

The other girls working in the boutique weren't surprised when Mr. Malone showed up either. They must have seen him so much by now that it was as normal as brushing your teeth every morning. I was still in awe with it all, and I'm sure in time it would be just as normal for me as well. Until then, I will keep my eyes open for his visits. I actually looked forward to seeing him for some reason.

Mr. Malone made the day more enjoyable, by just being in there. I must have had the same star stuck feelings the other women did when they saw him, I don't know, but until it becomes normal for me seeing him there as often as I do, I will have that same feeling as the other women do. Maybe.

CHAPTER 3

Summer went by pretty fast, and autumn was already making its presence known, with the drop in temperatures. The sky was turning with dark sinister clouds that gave off an eerie feeling each night. I knew I needed to get myself warmer clothes, and another blanket on the bed before long, but when the days were still on the warm side I put it off as long as I could. So far I hadn't had to turn the heat on, only because I prefer to sleep with it cooler at night, and I was toasty warm under the covers. The space heater in the bathroom did what it needed to in there when I took my bath, or shower, so I felt I was doing great. I had less than this many times while in foster care, so this was really a luxury for me.

Many of the outfits I chose to buy, had tights to match to keep my legs warm. I had been walking back and forth to work more often just because it gave me time to unwind before I reached home. I also enjoyed feeding the horse an apple on the way home, talking to him as if he could understand a single thing I was saying. The many secrets I told him knowing they wouldn't be repeated as well. I swear that horse knows my schedule pretty good, because it can be up at the stable when I walk out of the boutique, but by the time I reach the corner of the pasture, he's there waiting for me. I dubbed him Chestnut Charlie because of the beautiful chestnut color he was.

Business was slowing down a little, which concerned me that I would have my hours cut, but Molly said in November everything would pick back up with the holiday sales that start the day after Thanksgiving. I had nothing to worry about when I asked her about it.

I bought plenty of Halloween candy to pass out, only to find out someone had a big fall party at their house, and I had very few come to the porch to get candy. Later I learned it was Mr. Malone who had the party for everyone around that wanted to come. Guess it was a big deal every year, but I wasn't aware of it, and felt blind sided after spending so much on candy I was now stuck with.

Both Molly and I had been invited to Mr. Malone's house for Thanksgiving dinner. I wasn't sure he really invited me himself, but Molly insisted I go with her as her guest. I decided I'd go with Molly. The meal, and atmosphere was outstanding. Mary was a great cook, and everything was delicious. I stuffed myself full, and probably looked like a pig as I gobbled everything up, but no one mentioned it, or seemed to notice. Desserts were in abundance making it difficult to decide on which, but I settled on pumpkin pie with whip topping piled high.

Carrie Ann was present, as well as the ex-wife, Diana. Even though she was very cordial, she was a stuck up selfish snobbish person in my book. She barked orders to the staff, as if she was the one in charge still living there. Mary did a fantastic job putting her in her place several times that I had to chuckle to myself. Diana wasn't her boss, and she took nothing from her.

I just don't understand how an ex-wife can still be so bossy, and rude, towards everyone the way Diana was. What Diana wanted she felt she could get, and she did her best at getting it. I could tell she was use to getting her way at the time, and the way she looked down on people was disgusting, as far as I was concern.

Diana didn't have anything to prove to me, or anyone else anymore, but she still barked her orders as if she did. I believe she was the kind of person who only wanted you as a friend on her terms, and on her time. I bet she has dropped friends left and right when she felt they didn't conform to her way. Glad I kept my distance from her by staying close to Molly the entire time.

Carrie Ann was such a sweet girl that was going to turn seven on her next birthday. She resembled her father to a tee, and Diana wasn't happy about that either when Molly told Carrie Ann that. Diana wasn't very motherly towards Carrie Ann, but you could tell she wanted to be the center of attention all the time when people commented Carrie Ann on something she had done. Diana would jump in immediately to take the credit for Carrie Ann's achievement. How shallow could a person be?

Carrie Ann did resemble her dad very much, and she also had that same sadness in her eyes as Mr. Malone. However, she was a totally different little girl once her mother left. She must have been walking on egg shells around her mother all the time, and that is so wrong in my book. Made me wonder what Carrie Ann did in her mother's home differently from when she was at her father's place.

I felt so privileged when she asked if I would read a story to her. When I told her I would love to, her eyes brightened up, and a huge smile formed on her face. She ran to get a book, but I read only a few chapters of it before she fell asleep on my lap in the living room.

Mr. Malone came over scooping her up in his arms, carrying her to her room, and tucked her in for the night. Shortly, Molly and I excused ourselves to leave thanking Mr. Malone for his invitation for dinner. I stated that everything was absolutely delicious, adding that his daughter was a very sweet child. With the last part of my statement Mr. Malone actually had a warm smile spread across his face, which he then asked me to please call him Aaron.

～

The next day was very busy at the boutique, as Molly had said it would be. I was glad to see my shift end because my legs and back were killing me. I had a rough night trying to sleep the night before. That smile from Aaron kept creeping into my head. I didn't know what to think of it, but it kept me awake most of the night with happy thoughts racing around my brain.

Mary sent home several Tupperware containers full of food from yesterdays dinner. I was going to feast for days with the amount she sent home with both Molly and me. I wouldn't have to shop all this week for groceries, that was for sure. I knew I was in for a treat with my meals for several days to come.

I had taken a small Tupperware with me to work for lunch, and after I put it in the microwave, I couldn't wait to devour the delicious contents. Molly and I sat together at lunch in the tiny break room having lunch when a big ruckus in the store took Molly away.

Aaron had stopped in the store bringing Carrie Ann with him. He made his way back to the break room with Carrie Ann in hand. As soon as she saw me, she rushed over giving me the biggest bone crushing hug ever. She was full of bubbly chatter, and said she was so glad to see me again. Molly asked if I mind watching her, as Aaron and her had a few things to go over in the office.

I sure didn't mind one bit. I grabbed a paper plate from the cabinet giving Carrie Ann half the piece of pie I brought for dessert. Carrie Ann went on and on how much she loved pumpkin pie, but then added her mother won't let her eat it because it had a lot of sugar in it. Mary, however, would sneak her a piece when she could, and Carrie Ann thought that was the coolest thing ever. Maybe sharing my slice would rank me in her top favorites as well!

I didn't know if I should interrupt Molly and Aaron to seek permission before giving it to her, but decided against the interruption. Sometimes it's better, and easier, to ask forgiveness than for permission. I would take the consequences if I was wrong, but I didn't think I would be wrong if Mary gave her pieces of pie herself. It turned out I was right on that.

Carrie Ann was sad when it was time to leave. She wanted me to come to her house with them, so I could continuing to read the book to her again. I smiled telling her I would again sometime, but for now, I had to go back to work myself. Then, she added that she can see my house from her bedroom window.

How strange for Carrie Ann to say something like that. I knew there was no way she could see my little cottage from her bedroom window. She must think I live in the big house, and even then, I don't think she can see it with all the trees branches, and bushes, between our yards. I was curious as to why she would even look or let alone say it. Or maybe she was wishing she could. It didn't matter either way, if it made her feel better.

Once they had left, Molly and I sat in her office for awhile on a break just chit chatting. Molly brought up about Carrie Ann taking to me so quickly, and how different she acted when her mother wasn't present. Molly and I both thought she felt at ease when Diana wasn't around, like a little girl should. Kids are kids only for a short time before they become adults for the rest of their lives.

It seemed like our conversation was all about Aaron and Carrie Ann the entire break. Guess that was the only way I would learn anything more about them, was through Molly. It wasn't that I needed to know, but I wanted to know. I was intrigued with everything she said.

On my way home that night, I saw Chestnut Charlie headed my way, but this time Aaron was riding him. I was caught giving Chestnut Charlie an apple a few days earlier by one of the guys working in the stable who yelled at me. He must have reported it to Aaron. I was in trouble now, I thought.

Once Aaron realized it was me, he lost the angry look in

his face that I knew was there for whoever it was feeding his horse. I apologized for over stepping by giving his horse an apple without permission, but Aaron wasn't mad at all. In fact, he thought it was really kind of me. After I explained how his horse would greet me every day I walked home, he chuckled, telling me the horse was stalking me for a treat. We both laugh as if Chestnut Charlie understood, and shook his head left to right as to say *"no he wasn't."* The end of the pasture came, and Aaron turned Chestnut Charlie toward the stables, as I continued on my way home.

There was an alley separating the end of the pasture of Aaron's property, and Amber and Jonathan's land. Never went down the alley to see where it lead, but it was on my list to explore next. It caught my interest, after watching Aaron gallop away, to check it out. I had seen many cars drive by, but never knew where they were coming from, or going to. I honestly didn't think it was an actual alley, but there were plenty of cars that traveled it.

When I gathered the mail, there was a letter from the college Debbie attended. It was from the dean, of all people, with information that overwhelmed me. It also intrigued me that made me think maybe I should consider taking a class or two every semester when the next semester started, in January. It was something I had thought about while in high school, but my only goal at that time was to get out of that town as quick as I could. I also didn't think I had what it took to be in college. My grades were always good, but I wasn't in the group of people who went to college. Many people had it drilled into them from the time they were little to attend college, as if it was the next level of education that they were expecting to go, without any questions or qualms.

The following day I told Debbie about getting it, and that I thought maybe I would check it out. When Debbie offered to take me in mid-December, I gladly accepted, and was grateful for her offer. I had wanted to be a teacher ever since I could remember, and it may take me awhile, but I would try for it. I had nothing to lose, if the price was in my budget.

Debbie told me I would probably be able to get a grant since I didn't have anyone to pay for my education, and I lived on my own. I had never heard of a grant before, but if I could get one, it would help me tremendously. I talked to Molly about it later, and she was very supportive, and encouraged me to check it out. That was all I needed to hear, her approval. Why that was important, I don't know, but I didn't think Molly would ever steer me wrong.

With December being a week away we had to get the boutique changed to reflect the upcoming holiday. We didn't have the chance to do it during business hours so when Molly asked for volunteers to do it on Saturday night after hours, and Sunday during the day, I was right there offering my assistance. It was more than I thought it would be, but by the time Sunday evening came to an end, the place sparkled with lights taking on a festive look. I felt it myself, and that was a first for me.

Molly announced that this years Christmas dinner party would be at Aaron's on December 11th, and we were expected to attend. I gathered that this was a yearly thing everyone enjoyed very much. Apparently his house was decked to the hilt for Christmas, because he thought Christmas the best holiday of all. Not just for the holiday, but he always reached out to others during this time that couldn't go home, or didn't have any family to spend it with.

I hadn't thought about what I would be doing for Christmas very much, but I figured like the many holidays at Clara's, I'd be by myself in my room. No tree, no decorations, no holiday music, no exchange of gifts, no nothing. However, I was planning on getting a small artificial tree for my tiny house, and some holiday CD's to play. Now, I was determined to enjoy it all I could, thanks to the invitation to Aaron's house.

CHAPTER 4

Molly, Debbie, and I headed to the college to see what they could do for me on Saturday, and if I would qualify for a grant. We were going to make a day of it with lunch out as well.

I was really impressed with the campus, and the counselor that was helping me. Not only did she give me a sheet of the classes I would need to complete for my degree, but also helped me apply for the grants, to see what I might qualify for. All we had to do now is wait to see if I did qualify. If I do, I will be ready to take two evening classes when January semester starts. I knew which classes I wanted to take, and all I would have to do is call my counselor when, and if, I hear any news.

With that out of the way, the three of us went shopping for Christmas gifts, along with a dress to wear to Aaron's dinner party. I found a black velvet dress right away that was perfect for me, and within my budget. It was stylish, and fitted very nice on me. The neckline was a little lower than what I am accustom to, but not as low as to show all my business either. Many of the beautiful dresses I looked at were so expensive that I would have loved to have purchased, but I knew my limits, and I didn't want to budge from it. I had black velvet heels I could wear with it, so I was set. Molly found a red dress she looked fabulous in, and Debbie chose a gold glittery dress, which I thought would be more appropriate for New Years Eve party. It had a very plunging neckline that did show her business in my opinion. I may be old fashion, but I knew what her game was all the same. She liked attracting attention from everyone and anyone.

Once we were done dress shopping, we had lunch at this cute little diner with the best cheese burgers I have ever tasted. I don't go out to lunch often, but this was a special day for us. First, my possibility of going to college, second was getting my first real party dress ever, and lastly, I was with two people I considered my friends. I was in a different frame of mind since coming to Jasper, and it was a great feeling to have all these wonderful things finally happening to me.

The following weekend we would be enjoying ourselves at Aaron's dinner party, and I was looking forward to that eagerly. I just had to get through the week at work in the boutique, where it was plain out crazy with shoppers, and doing the main house cleaning. I was exhausted when I would get home, but somehow managed to get my second wind as I walked in the door of my home.

The days were pretty chilly, the sun was out brightly, and so far no signs of any snow. The sky fooled me on many occasions though. It looked as if the purple clouds would burst open any minute, allowing snowflakes to float down to earth. It never happened though.

I made sure I was bundled warm when I was outside. I surely didn't drag my feet getting to work, or back home either. Chestnut Charlie never failed to meet me at the start of my walk along the fence home. The stableman would smile, and wave to me now, as I fed Chestnut Charlie his daily apple. At least he wasn't running to Aaron to report about me anymore. I made sure to wave back, and give him a smile. He was only doing his job, although I had taken it personal at first.

My little Christmas tree was decorated from top to bottom, as it stood proudly on the little table in front of my living room window. No one could see it from any other direction, but that didn't matter to me. I saw it, and it warmed my soul. While I prepared my little dinner, I had Christmas carols playing on my CD player. I would either sing along, or hum while making my meal. I was happy, and nothing but nothing, could change that.

I watched the evening news after dinner, especially the weather. I needed to know in advance what I could expect the following day. Then usually a movie before my shower and bed. It was such a routine anymore, but I didn't mind. Besides, there were several Christmas movies I had never seen, and found them very enjoyable.

I had a letter from the college waiting for me Saturday afternoon when I arrived home. I was so apprehensive to open it. I received the grant for the semester for two classes and supplies I would need. I was jumping up and down in the driveway. I noticed Miss. Nelson was staring at me through her window. I smiled, and waved at her. She disappeared so fast. If only she knew what was going on in my life, but I didn't care who saw me, I was happy!

I followed the alley one afternoon when it was warm enough outside, and it led right to Aaron's driveway. It was like a driveway where he could escape from the front gate, with all the women standing there waiting to get a glimpse of him. I had to chuckle, but at the same time, I knew I could walk there for the dinner party without having to walk all the way around his property to get to the front door.

I finished my cleaning in the main house in record time, as well as my own laundry, before I decided to take a long soak in the tub before getting ready to go to Aaron's. I purchased a bottle of fine wine to take as a token of his kindness, and appreciation. Why was wine so expensive I don't know, but I was shocked when I purchased it. I had asked Molly to suggest a good wine assuming she knew why, and hopefully told me Aaron's preference. Blew my budget there on one purchase in one single store, so I hope he'll appreciate it.

⌒

I arrived at the same time Molly was getting out of her car, so we entered the mansion together. I just stood there at the doorway gawking at the beauty of everything. The Christmas trees were absolutely huge. All were gorgeous with all the lights, ornaments, and all the other holiday items displayed in the rooms. I knew Christmas was his favorite holiday, but I never expected to see the inside decorated as perfect as his home was. Every tree ornament was meticulously placed, and with the lights reflecting off them, made an illusion of more lights, and more color with the reflection from the huge mirrors.

Aaron came over to greet us, as the butler took our coats. He leaned in to kiss Molly on the check, and when it came to me he whispered in my ear I "was absolutely stunning" before kissing my cheek. I knew I had to have blushed as red as Molly's dress from the heat I could feel in my face. I was on cloud nine from there on for the rest of the evening. No one could bust my personal bubble I had going on in my head.

I mumbled something on the line of how beautiful his house was, as I handed him the bottle of wine. He smiled telling me I didn't have to, but he appreciated it by thanking me kindly. It wasn't long before Carrie Ann saw me, and ran over to greet me. She looked so adorable in her outfit that was fit for a princess. I knew right away Diana wasn't there from Carrie Ann's happiness, and was glad of that. Carrie Ann could be herself as she made her rounds to greet all the guests. She was a pint sized hostess that knew exactly what to do.

Once everyone was there from the boutique, we were taken into the dining room where we were seated. I somehow managed to be seated on the right side of Aaron, and Carrie Ann on his left. Molly winked smiling at me as she sat down next to me. I knew we were going to have a talk later on about this, but for now, I was enjoying everything.

Dinner was the most delicious meal with three courses served. I was delighted with every bite I took, and the desserts were beyond what I had ever seen or tasted before in my life. I was very impressed with everything you could say. I never knew people could live, and eat like this in a million years, but I was part of it tonight. I was basking in it totally as if it was a normal thing for me.

After dinner we all gathered in the living room as a cart of gifts was guided in by Mary. I didn't think anything could top this evening, but was I mistaken. Molly gave a speech she had prepared thanking Aaron for opening his beautiful home to us, and how much she appreciated each and everyone of us working for her.

One by one, she called us up to receive her token of appreciation in a gift from her. When my name was called, I glanced at Aaron, and he had such a warmness in him as he smiled at me. He definitely knew how to make me blush. I was just hoping I wouldn't stumble at any point.

I thanked Molly for my gift, and walked back to where the rest of my co-workers were standing. Debbie nudged me, and I asked if this was a normal thing that is done. She affirmed that it was. She even said not to open it until I was by myself, which I thought was rather strange, but I took her advise, and would open it at a later time.

Molly joined Debbie, and myself, where I thanked her again for my gift. She told me she has the best group of people working for her, and she appreciates each of us.

After awhile, everyone started to excuse themselves to leave. I noticed the time, and knew I needed to get home as well. I never intended to stay this long, but time just flew by so fast. I don't like walking into my place after dark, but I left my tree lights on with the music playing. I thanked Molly and Aaron again, before I said my good-byes to everyone, and slipped out the door only to scoot around to the back alley to walk home. I was too embarrassed to ask anyone for a ride, it was really cold, so I walked as fast as I could.

I reached the little opening between overgrown bushes to the backyard of my home. My little Christmas tree was proudly shining through the window, and I knew I would soon be warm, and safe inside. As I went to unlock my door, I looked over to Aaron's house to see if they could see my place from there, and they couldn't. The trees were bare of their leaves, and I knew they could see the big house for sure.

I was glad to get inside warming my feet, hands, and face before getting ready for bed. I was going to sleep well, as I snuggled deep under the blanket and quilt. I was toasty warm, as I drifted off to sleep rather quickly.

I was having some of the best dreams ever, until one was about Aaron. I popped my eyes open, bolting into a upright sitting position so fast making sure I was dreaming. What was going on with me, I couldn't explain. Was it the whisper in my ear from Aaron, or the kiss on my cheek that sent me into that dream. I don't know, but I liked it anyhow. How could I talk about this to anyone? I couldn't tell them that was the very first time a guy told me I looked stunning, let alone the very first time a guy has kissed me, even though it was just on the cheek. That thought alone left me warm inside, as I fell back asleep hoping the dream would continue.

I slept in late the following morning for the first time in months. I deserved it. I had all my work done in the main house, my laundry done, my own place clean, and had the day to do whatever I wanted. That felt good too! I watched a Christmas movie in the afternoon, while eating a large bowl of buttered popcorn, that I had always wanted to watch. I was content with everything, and enjoyed my day.

I placed my gift from Molly under my little tree when I got home, knowing I would have something to open Christmas morning, for the first time in many years. I was feeling very blessed.

CHAPTER 5

My little decorated Christmas tree looked so sad with the one, and only present under it, but it was better than nothing under it at all. It was still in the decorated holiday bag, but I could peek inside to find there was a envelope. Most likely a gift card, or cash. I was determined not to bother it until Christmas morning.

Work was a complete zoo with everyone shopping for their holiday gifts. I was more than ready to leave when my shift was over. My head was always pounding from the noise, music, and chatter from the people. It seemed like one person had to be so loud, and another person had to top that noise level every single day. I didn't mean to sound so negative, because everyone was in the spirit of the holiday, but I was just plain tired.

Molly beamed from ear to ear when the day was done, and she rang up the sales tape. She was very pleased with the amounts she saw. A few nights we went out for a bite to eat after work, and I was really glad I didn't have to prepare anything for myself.

Molly knew there was something on my mind, and she was trying to ease her way to that.

I finally asked her if she knew why Aaron placed me next to him at the Christmas dinner party, and not her. I felt she should have been the one sitting next to him. She smiled, stating she had no clue, but said it was always an honor to be the one sitting next to him. There was something about her answer that made me drop the topic, and just leave it to chance. Maybe I was putting more thought into it than what it actually was, I don't know, but I liked it.

Molly did say that we were invited to have Christmas dinner at his house as well. I don't like it when I'm not asked directly, and it sure makes me feel like I'm a third wheel. I told her I had to think about that, even though I knew I had nothing else planned for that day other than popping a TV turkey dinner into the microwave. I thought it would be great to go one minute, and angry the next. Aaron doesn't have to go through Molly to ask me, or tell me that I'm invited there. I didn't know how to read his invitation through Molly, or was it Molly that really was inviting me. It made me feel uncomfortable either way.

Sure enough, the very next day Aaron came in to the boutique himself, walking directly to Molly's office. He didn't seem very chipper either, so something wasn't going right. I kept my eye on the door to see what he looked like when he was leaving.

When he came out, he looked directly at me, catching my eye. Smiling, he walked over to me asking if we could talk a few minutes. It was then, that he invited me to Christmas dinner at his house, as if he had overheard my thoughts earlier. He was having a small group of people, which were his employees and their families. I accepted his invitation then, asking if I could bring anything. After that came out of my mouth, I felt foolish for even asking, since he has all these other people working for him. His reply was kind though, by telling me to bring an empty stomach, because the meal was going to be big before he turned and left.

Debbie came over to me right after Aaron had left, asking if everything was alright. I quietly told her Aaron had just invited me to Christmas dinner. The grin on her face was so sly, and she had the "hmm hmm hmm" in her voice that made me think she had something reeling in her mind over that. She smiled so coyly, as she walked back to her register. I couldn't tell her it was nothing, because maybe it was the beginning of something that I didn't even know. Or, just wishful thinking on my part. Or, was she jealous he hadn't invited her when I thought about how she was at the Christmas party around him in her gold glittery dress. I think she was trying to get his attention in every way possible.

Before I started my walk home, I ran next door to the grocery store where I bought a beautiful poinsettia plant to take over to Miss. Nelson, as a kind holiday gift. I really wanted to be a good neighbor, but she wasn't making it easy. I purchased an apple for Chestnut Charlie at the same time, and was soon on my way out the door.

Chestnut Charlie ran to the pasture fence to greet me as soon as he saw me. It didn't take him long to devour that apple once I gave it to him. He walked along the fence with me to the end, as I talked the entire way before he departed heading to the stable.

I walked up the sidewalk to Miss Nelson's house, and on to her wrap around porch. When I reached the door, I was hoping she would answer, but she didn't. I should have known she wouldn't when I think about it. I left the poinsettia on the porch by the door, and was walking to my home disappointed she hadn't answered. I was sure I heard the front door open, so I stopped. Looking over to her house, I couldn't believe what I saw with my own two eyes. She kicked the plant right off her porch, and slammed her door shut. I stood in my driveway with my eyes huge, and mouth gapping open at what I had just witnessed.

How rude could someone be! What an ungrateful scrooge! I quickly wanted to give her a piece of my mind. I marched over to her sidewalk leading to the porch, but decided when I saw the poor plant laying on the ground, that I would just take my gift back. Miss Nelson could rot in her misery, as far as I was concerned. The plant surely didn't need to be kicked away as it had been. I scooped as much soil up as possible, as I placed it back in the pot, taking it home with me. I would love it myself, if it wasn't too late, or it didn't die from the cold ground.

I told Molly the next day over lunch what I had done, and what had happened with Miss Nelson. She said Miss Nelson is the most unfriendly person known to mankind. A scorned bitter divorced woman that hates everyone, and everything.

Miss Nelson was bitterly frigid cold as the Arctic ice in winter Molly continued on. Her husband had stuck it out for over three years in a heartless marriage before he decided it wasn't worth the time trying any longer, and filed for divorce. Once that happened, and the divorce was final, she closed off her life to anyone else. She also returned to her maiden name.

Miss Nelson tried using her house as a bed and breakfast, to show the people around her she was a good solid person, who had been done wrong by her horrible husband. However, her guest weren't pleased with what was going on either. Many left during the middle of the night without paying, which made Miss Nelson even more bitter, claiming her ex-husband was the one who caused her failed business venture when he had nothing to do with it.

Sad to think she had so much hate in herself that she made it impossible to enjoy the rest of her life. She couldn't move on, and didn't want anyone else to either. Molly never said how she knew this information, but she was pretty accurate in telling it.

Molly's family was the first family to settle in Jasper. Molly had so much information on everything historical happening during that time. Her family was very important in the town, and their businesses flourished tremendously. In fact, Aaron's house was the first house ever built in Jasper, and it belonged to Molly's grandparents. Molly lived in the mansion herself, once her grandparents passed on.

The family graves are located on the property towards the back of the garage where all the grandparents through the family tree are buried. I planned on going to the library, and get books on the area to learn more.

Lunch was over, and I needed to get back out in the boutique. I thought what an interesting lunch I had. History was right up my alley. I was always wanting to learn as much as I could on anything historical. Probably why I wanted to become a History teacher, to pass the information on to young minds.

As I was walking home with Chestnut Charlie walking along the other side of the fence munching on his apple, I tried to envision what the street was like in the beginning of Jasper, and all I could see was lots of huge mansions with everyone getting along to enjoy life. Kids would be playing in many yards, and for sure there were many front porch visits after dinner with neighbors. Yep, I was a dreamer for sure.

I quickly shut the door behind me before letting in any cold weather, once I stepped inside my home. Put on water to heat for a cup of tea, and flipped the TV on. I listened to the news as I prepared my leftover food hoping I'd hear something good in the world, but it seemed full of glum and dismay. Glad to watch another movie as I ate my supper.

Molly closed early on Christmas Eve so everyone could get home to start their holiday, but there were those late last minute shoppers that had to come in at the very last minute. I offered to stay while the others left until the very last customer finally left. Glad to shut the lights off and lock the door, I started my journey home, when I heard Aaron call my name as I crossed the street.

I turned my head towards the sound of sleigh bells, and Aaron's voice, as Chestnut Charlie, hitched to a sleigh, pulled up next to me. Carrie Ann was bouncing up and down with shear delight, and Aaron invited me to go with them for a ride around the neighborhood to look at the houses all decorated with the many lights and decorations.

I couldn't deny the chance of that, as Aaron extended his hand to help me into the sleigh. Carrie Ann threw open the quilts for me to cover up with next to her, and her father. Benny, from the stable, was holding the reigns directing Chestnut Charlie along the streets.

So many homes were so beautifully decorated. I must have been staring at them with wide eyes as Carrie Ann. I had never seen such a sight as I was on that sleigh ride. Everything was so beautiful, and I felt so blessed to be seeing it with Aaron and Carrie Ann.

It was an absolute wonderful evening, and as cold as it was, I felt warm and comfortable. I was glad to have been invited along, and no one knew it was the first time looking at other people's lighted houses for me. We stopped next to the park, and Aaron pulled a thermos out from under the covers on the floor, and poured the four of us hot chocolate. Aaron handed me my mug, and quietly told me he was very happy I was with them. I smiled thanking him for this wonder surprise. As we sipped on the hot chocolate, and nibbled from a tin filled to the top with Mary's holiday cookies, Carrie Ann was busy talking about what she hoped Santa would be bringing her. She had asked Santa at the mall for a few things, but she had one wish she couldn't tell anyone. She had a twinkle in her eyes as she talked about it.

I thanked Aaron again, as I was dropped off in front of the house. Told Carrie Ann I'd see her, and everyone else tomorrow for dinner. Aaron offered to walk me to my door, but I told him to stay warm under the quilts, and made my way to my little house.

I smiled as I heard the sleigh turn down the alley towards

the stables with the bells tingling along. I glanced over to the break in the bushes watching them as they went by. It was a great evening, and I enjoyed it very much. Carrie Ann was hoping for snow tonight, and I was too. I wanted a white Christmas for her, and for myself, being my first Christmas in Jasper.

I slept so well that night thinking of the evening as I closed my eyes. I woke up to a racket outside my window. I got up to see Miss Nelson throwing out boxes of something which I didn't know of what, but she sure was tossing something. She wasn't displaying any happiness from the look on her face. Well, Merry Christmas to you…even if you'll never know I wished it.

One thing I did notice, no snow yet, but I could see many chimney releasing smoke into the air, so I knew it was plenty cold outside. I can only image the kids excitement for the anticipation of Santa's arrival.

~

Was I ever surprised when I woke up to the many inches of snow that had fallen. It had to have been at least ten inches already. Both Carrie Ann and I had that wish come true. I climbed out of bed making myself a cup of tea, turned on my CD player for Christmas music, and made my way over to my tree to open my one and only gift under it. I opened the package pulling out the envelope Molly had placed inside. I couldn't believe my eyes when I saw her letter written on the card with a $100 bill falling into my lap. $100!! I have never ever had a gift in my entire life like that.

I read the note Molly had written, and felt tears run down my cheeks. I didn't know what to say to her when I saw her later, but I knew she would be getting a hug from me for sure, for the money, and for what she had written. I was at a loss for words for myself, and that has never happened before!

CHAPTER 6

C hristmas dinner was what I had expected it to be, and more. I sat to the right of Aaron again, and Carrie Ann to his left, as we had done the month previously. The entire staff was included with their family members making it was the most joyful dinner I had ever been to. The center pieces were tall vases with miniature poinsettias surrounding a white tapered candle. Very beautiful, very festive, and very elegant.

Once dinner was over, everyone gathered in the family room where Molly played the piano, and everyone sang one Christmas carol after another, before they started to leave for their own homes. I watched them enjoy themselves thinking how I had never had a Christmas quite like this one.

Once everyone was gone, Aaron asked if I'd like a tour of the home. I blurted out, "you bet", without realizing how eager I had been to see what else I could. He chuckled taking my hand showing me his office first. I was blown away with the detail and furnishings he had. Several large photos of the town in the beginning stage of Jasper. It was amazing to see each photo while reading all the captions under each.

Aaron had several shelves of books on display. I recognized several books that he wrote, but didn't realize he had written as many as he had.

Some of the books looked very old, and he said they were first editions of the town establishment of the founding fathers and families. He said any time I wanted to borrow one I was welcome, but I would worry about ruining them by accident, so I'd better stick to the library for that. At his desk where he wrote his books was surrounded by floor to ceiling windows, and French doors, with many plants flourishing from the sunlight the windows provided.

He had access to three sides of the yard through the many French doors. I saw that there was a swimming pool in the backyard, covered for the winter months, view of the entire pasture from behind his desk, and the front yard on the other side where I noticed he could see the plaza across the street.

Above the huge fireplace was a portrait of a man, which I learned was Jasper Malone himself. Very distinguished looking man with kind eyes. Aaron told me every boy in the family has carried Jasper as their middle name since then, which I thought was really a cool thing to carry on the family legacy like that.

The dark mahogany wood and bookcases, were elegant. I knew someone had great taste and money, to be able to purchase such an item many years ago. The leather couch and loveseat were set in front of the fireplace, making the room more than just a work space for Aaron, but a place that felt comfortable and peaceful.

Aaron had a Christmas tree by the fireplace decorated and lighted, like the others in the rest of the house, with several poinsettia plants all along the hearth. It looked like the ornaments were very old ones. Aaron explained they were from the first Christmas tree his great great grandparents, Jasper and Amanda, had.

A grandfather clock chimed midnight, and I realized I needed to get myself home. The rest of the house tour would have to wait. Now, I'm not Cinderella needing to get home before everything changes as it did for her, but I was getting tired, and knew it was time to leave. Aaron offered to drive me home which I declined telling him I could walk the short distance through the alley behind his house.

He retrieved my coat, holding it open for me to put on, and quickly put his on as he decided he could at least walk me home. It was so quiet and peaceful outside, with snow slowly making its way to the ground again. I slipped on the ice, and Aaron quickly grabbed me to steady me. He continued to hold my hand the rest of the way to the break between the bushes, where we parted way. I thanked him once again for the wonderful evening, and as I started to walk away, he quickly kissed my cheek saying he'd wait for me to get inside my home before leaving. I turned walking towards my house with the biggest smile across my face, and a fluttering heart.

Once I got to my door, I opened it and waved good bye to Aaron. Continuing inside where it was toasty warm, and placed my hand over my beating heart. I was over the moon with happiness.

Trying to fall asleep wasn't easy, and when I finally did, it was one dream after another of Aaron. I was content not wanting to wake myself up.

⌒

It was only a few days later, when I saw Aaron go into Molly's office again. He looked across the store until he found me, and smiled before he went inside. I didn't see him leave, and I was surprised how that had upset me. I was looking for all the small times I did see him to only get a smile or a wave of the hand, but when I didn't get one this time, I wondered what was up which put myself into a salty mood for awhile.

A few weeks passed by before I saw Aaron come into the store again. I flashed him a big smile, but either he didn't see me, or he was ignoring me. Either way my heart sank, as I struggled to finish out my shift in a positive mood. I really think either I'm putting more into how I feel about Aaron than necessary, or there wasn't anything special between us like I thought.

I no sooner walked into my house when there was a knock at the door, and it was Aaron. He was very apologetic for just showing up at my door, but he didn't have a way to call in advance. I invited him in as he explained Molly had told him I didn't have a phone, so he took a chance by just stopping as he did. I didn't think anything bad about it, and offered him a cup of coffee, or tea. That was then he took a small box out of his coat pocket handing it to me.

What a surprise for me, a cell phone which he had put his private number in under AJ, his house number under Malone, and Molly's private number with her business number as well. He told me this way he would be able to call me at any time, and we could talk later at night when I was home, and we wouldn't be interrupted.

How very sweet, but I wondered why he thought I needed Molly's numbers in that phone with his. I didn't think it was something I really needed, yet wondered why. What was it between the two of them? Molly was a very nice person that I admired greatly, but she was included with everything all the time. Was there more to this friendship than I saw? I didn't have the nerve to ask either. Just be grateful, and accept the phone graciously, which I did.

Aaron had to get back to his house to have dinner with Carrie Ann. Mary was there until he got back from running over to see me. I understood completely, and he kissed my cheek as he left.

It wasn't two minutes later, my phone rang for the first time. It was Aaron, and he thanked me for taking the phone, because he really wanted to be able to talk with me more often. My heart was pounding so hard against my chest thinking he did have some kind of feelings for me. He was home and ready to eat his dinner, so we said our goodbyes, until later.

~

I had started my classes at college, and enjoyed them. Only two nights a week, but the classes were three hours long, and at times very stuffy. It was that night I struggled to keep my mind focused on what was being said. When our class was over, I think I was the first to the door to get out. I had to take the city bus, because I didn't have a vehicle, but I knew it was only a short drive to my stop.

I had Chestnut Charlie waiting for me at the end of his pasture to walk with me every time, and he was happy to get his apple. Within a minute, my phone was already ringing. Aaron was just checking to see if I was okay, and how my class had gone. I talked with him until I opened my door, and was safely inside.

It was still several weeks before Molly and I had a chance to talk, but I knew I wanted to talk to her. Everything was going by so fast, we hadn't even sat long for a break by ourselves, but she did tell me Aaron had a new novel coming out soon. Molly was planning a signing gig at the store in two weeks. Why didn't Aaron tell me that himself?

There were cases upon cases of additional books being delivered, with no place to store them other than in the back room, which we referred to as the dungeon. It was always dark, and creepy, back there. I dreaded every time I had to go in there. But, I had to go there plenty of times through the day lately, so I had to get over the fear I had.

Molly also dropped the news that Aaron would be out of town for the next three or four weeks traveling to go to book stores promoting his book. She had such a worried look on her face, and it didn't seem like she was happy about something, or was very upset. Either way, she didn't find it necessary to discuss it with me. I bet she discussed it with Aaron though!

I was taken back by her actions too. I didn't know if I had done or said something to upset her, but I was taking her coolness very personal. I decided to keep my distance, and just do my work.

When the week came to get everything set up for Aaron's book signing, I noticed Molly had several posters made announcing the signing event that I had to display in the windows. She realized she ordered too many, and decided maybe she could just give the customers one until they were gone. I snatched one up myself taking it home with me and that night tacking it to the wall in my bedroom. It was a very good photo of Aaron, and I wasn't going to miss out on getting one of them.

The day came for the book signing. Molly had asked if anyone would volunteer to work later that Friday night setting up, and Saturday for the book signing itself, which I did. Molly needed someone to make sure there were plenty of books up front, and asked me to man the register. It was a packed crowd that came in Saturday, and not just for a few hours, it was all day long! In two days time we emptied out four large cases of his books, and sales were out of this world.

Molly seemed a little relieved, but she still had that distant look about her. I finally asked to speak with her in private after closing, if that was possible, to address the elephant in the room.

I was right, she was upset, and was having a hard time dealing with everything. She didn't say what it was, but it had nothing to do with me at all. She hadn't realized I was able to detect her change in mood, but glad I brought it to her attention.

Apparently, Diana was up to her games again making threats to hold Aaron from seeing Carrie Ann, if he didn't increase her child support. Diana was so greedy, and knowing the new book released, she knew he had more money he could part with. She knew how to play her game using Carrie Ann as her pawn.

Diana hired an attorney, and the court date was approaching in a few weeks. Aaron wasn't happy either, because Diana made other demands and accusations against Aaron. Diana was so sure Aaron had another woman sleeping with him already, which she didn't like when her daughter was staying there. She was going to make his life miserable any way she could.

That explained everything about her actions, and Aaron's as well. It had to be hard to meet the demands of an out of reach woman, as Diana seems to be. I didn't know the extent of her demands, but they had to be something big from the way Aaron and Molly were acting. I could understand Aaron being out of sorts with life at the moment, but why was Molly so upset? Was there a reason why Molly took it personally as well? I don't know why, but it struck strange with me. Did it have to do with me having a phone, and talking nightly with Aaron? I had kept the phone quiet as he had asked, not telling anyone about having it. What was the problem?

After the signing Aaron and Molly headed to her office closing the door behind them. I finished putting the extra table and few books on the shelf away before clocking out for home. It had been a long and tiring day, and I was ready to relax.

As soon as I got home, I grabbed a mug of coffee from my kitchen going to my swing to wind down once I had the chimera lit to keep warm with, when I looked up and saw Aaron coming through the opening in the bushes. He wasn't looking as tired as he had been, as he walked over to me he was actually smiling. I knew it was okay for me to relax then. I ran in to get him a mug of coffee, and we talked for hours as the night grew shorter.

Aaron wanted to get to know me better, as he spoke in such a soothing voice.

Before I knew it, I was spilling my soul to him. Our nightly phone talks were so generic, but I enjoyed them none the less. Now I was spilling out my life growing up in the foster system, not knowing my parents, landing both the jobs I have that I love so much, living in my own little house on my own, my travel to get here, to just about anything that popped into my mind. Then as soon as I blurted everything out, I realized I said too much. More than what I had ever wanted anyone to know of me. I was angry with myself for letting go as I did. How did Aaron have that effect on me, I don't know.

Aaron sensed something happened between the last statement to that moment, and he moved closer to me telling me he was glad I opened up to him. He wanted to know more about me, but there wasn't any more to say, so I just asked him to share his life with me in return. I didn't think he would, but he started out slowly at first, and then it was wham, more information than what I had expected.

Aaron was raised by his grandparents after his parents had died in a small plane crash coming back from skiing in the mountains. He had been too young to go with them, but his older brother and sister were old enough. They also died in the crash. His whole family was wiped out a mere two miles from here, in the wooded area along the property line. He didn't understand what had happened at first, because he was so young, but he was soon living with his grandparents in the same house he is living in now.

His grandparents made sure they kept him busy. He

excelled in school allowing him to graduate high school two years earlier, and off he went to college. He missed his family greatly having a hard time being away, so he decided to go to college in the next town where he would be able to be in his own home, and bedroom every night. He started out thinking he wanted to be a journalist, but changed his goal to writing books instead. That was where he ended, still doing to this day, and loving every moment of it. His grandfather had told him to do something he has a passion with, and it will never seem like work he "had" to do.

While in his last year of college, he met Diana, and thought she was the one he wanted to be with forever. He was almost twenty at the time, and had never experienced love before. Diana was the first to pay attention to him, and he was thrilled with the concept of having a girlfriend. He was so in love, but now realize it wasn't love, it was just the idea he had a girlfriend, a full blown fantasy he was having. He graduated that Spring, and by June they were married. It was too fast for him, but she was so insistent that he went along with everything she wanted. She also informed him she was pregnant making things worse.

They married in June, and later that year Carrie Ann was born. Things started to change. Diana didn't like the responsibility of caring for a child, and after a few years, she didn't want anything more to do with Carrie Ann at all. She wanted everything to be about her, and started acting like a teenager going clubbing almost every night with her friends. One argument after another started until she stated she wanted her space, but not a divorce.

She moved to her own room in the house, coming and going as she pleased. His grandparents weren't happy with what was going on, and after a year of her nonsense, his grandfather implored him to seek a divorce, which he did.

Diana went completely crazy, spewing vile accusations at his grandparents, friends, and told him she would get Carrie Ann, cleaning him out of every penny to his name. She had the nerve to tell him she had only married him for his wealth, and her plan to have Carrie Ann was part of making sure she would get everything she wanted.

The divorce was a very ugly one. The media ate it up making him look like a horrible person, stating he had tarnished the family name making Diana a slave in his home. He assured me he had never done that, as there were plenty of hired help to do all the work so she wouldn't have to lift a finger on anything, including taking care of Carrie Ann.

His divorce took months to finalize, and he was granted custody of Carrie Ann for all the holidays, weekends, and summers. Diana would have her only for the school days along with a hefty alimony check for five years, and child support for Carrie Ann. She was striped of the Malone name. He was devastated, and after he signed the agreement he thought it would be over, but it wasn't.

If it hadn't been for the support of the family, especially his grandparents, he would have lost everything. His heart had been broken, and he never thought it would be mended again. Carrie Ann was the best thing from that marriage, and he loved her immensely. He had to survive for her, and he made it his goal to be the best loving father to her.

Shortly after the divorce, his grandfather had taken ill, and died within a few weeks. It hit Aaron extremely hard. His only male figure in his life that was his rock for advice, and understanding. Aaron knew it wasn't just life that was hard for his grandfather, but his age, and poor health was against him.

He was fourteen years older than his grandmother providing for her very well, and he also had gone through a nasty divorce himself, which was something Aaron had never known until he was going through his own divorce. His grandfather had told him he would meet someone who would change his mind on love and life again, like he had, and be happy to the end of the time that he was given on earth.

Aaron was glad for his grandfather's advice, but it was still hard when he passed away. Aaron said his grandfather lived long enough to see him through the divorce, but wished he was still around now to see where he is in life now. That was when Aaron decided to step up, and care for his grandmother, for his grandfather.

Aaron was able to write the stories he did because they were all about what he lacked in love, and longed for. Not in the exact way his characters found love, but what he thought they should feel. His stories came from his broken heart.

I was more than happy to hear of his life, but after a pause in the sharing, we changed the subject matter talking about simple things, like what we wanted in life, favorite colors, seasons of the years, holidays, and the such. Back to the generic topics. Generic, but safe topics.

When he asked if I had a boyfriend I told him no. I had never been on a date, to a dance, out to dinner, nothing, nothing, nothing.

He shook his head remarking if I've never had a boyfriend, have I ever been kissed before by a guy? Embarrassed, I chuckled telling him the closest I've been kissed was by him, when he kissed my cheeks at his house the times I was invited for dinner.

He turned my face towards him with his hands cupping my face, and said he thought he needed to rectify that, and make my first kiss memorable. And that he did. And the second kiss was even better with the third one better yet.

CHAPTER 7

I slept so well through the night after Aaron left, which was actually after three this morning. Getting to know him was enlightening, and he trusted me enough to tell me information he may not have shared with many others. I didn't feel as bad telling him what a misfortune I have had growing up afterwards. I do know that my feelings for Aaron are true feelings, but I long to know more about him in every way possible.

I opened my door to let the sun shine in, to find a bud vase with a beautiful red rose in it on my sidewalk outside the door. Aaron had been by already, and left it there for me, knowing I'd find it as soon as I opened my door. It was such a sweet gesture, and the rose's fragrance was absolutely wonderful. A note was attached that he had to go into town for something. He'd would be back later, and would see me then if he could. I smiled knowing then I hadn't scared him off.

After fixing breakfast for myself, I set out to finish my own house cleaning and laundry when I heard Aaron's knock on my door. He was back earlier than I expected carrying a bag holding sub sandwiches for us, asking if I could come over to his place to eat them, and swim in the pool. Everyone was off for the day, and it would only be us.

It didn't take me long to change into my swimsuit, pull a tee shirt and shorts on over it, and we made our way to his house. He had a small side table set up outside with iced tea in a pitcher, and glasses ready to be filled, as we ate pool side. It was a gorgeous day.

We sat back on the double lounge talking, while sipping our tea. Aaron was relieved he hadn't scared me away last night, or that he was pushing me into seeing him more than what I wanted. He was genuinely concerned of my feelings, and when I told him I wasn't scared, or turned off, he slid me closer to him where he kissed me again. He revealed something that really made my heart pump fast right then.

He had noticed me my very first day I started working for Molly, but he had been so burned by Diana in their marriage he wasn't going to take the leap of getting burned again, and kept his distance. He had built a stone wall around his heart, and every time he saw me, a stone fell to the ground. That was over a year ago. I never knew. Even though it had been five years since his divorce, he was gun shy on meeting anyone, and have any feelings.

He found what information he wanted about me through Molly, who didn't know much other than I was a great worker, and always there to help when asked. I was house sitting Jonathan's house living in the in-law suite out back, and it appeared I didn't have any family or boyfriend, because I never mentioned anyone to her. He was very curious making several more visits to see Molly, just so he could get a chance at seeing me.

That explained why he was always in Molly's office talking, he was pumping her for information on me. On Me! I was very flattered knowing this now, but it still didn't explain why Molly was at every function of Aaron's.

The invites to dinner at his house was his way to get to see me more, without only getting the short glimpses he could only get at the boutique. He liked what he saw very much.

I liked what I saw, what I heard, and what I was feeling for him. There was no denying I was head over heels in love with Aaron, but couldn't tell him in words. Not yet. He would have to tell me how he felt first, and I was hoping it wouldn't be too long.

We talked for so long that the sun was blocked behind the dark clouds forming. A storm was about to let loose on us. We quickly grabbed everything running to get inside, but not before the rain came pouring down.

Aaron suggested a movie in the office, and we stayed there while the storm made its presence known loud and clear on the outside. I felt Aaron slide closer to me on the leather couch pulling me into his arms kissing me where we left off the night before. Long passionate kisses that left me wanting for more, and not just more kisses.

I slid down on the couch as Aaron slid next to me. Our kisses got very intense as the feelings in my body grew out of control, and craved him. I wanted to satisfy those cravings when he lifted my tee shirt up putting his hand around my breast. I thought I was going to explode. I moaned out loud pressing myself into him never wanting to let go. Aaron was so gentle, and if this was a part of making love, I knew I was in heaven. I didn't stop him, but he withdrew his hand and sat up quickly.

I was bewildered and now embarrassed. He whispered he was sorry that he was going too fast and wanted to slow things down, stating I would have to be the one that would let things go further if I was ready, and only when I was ready. He could and would wait for me to give him a sign that it was time. But not right now. I needed to process my feelings, and emotions more. I was bewildered laying there not knowing what to do or say.

I understood in one aspect, but I also wanted him to go on right now. I didn't want to wait. No sooner as I thought that, Molly came in with Carrie Ann in tow. Carrie Ann was excited seeing me there that Aaron and I didn't get a chance to talk anymore alone.

I walked home by myself that night feeling confused, and even felt a little slutty for wanting more from Aaron right then. Also, for allowing myself to let go of my inhibitions on love. When I climbed in bed, I was drained from all the thoughts and emotions I was dealing with, and fell asleep. I didn't sleep much, just tossed and turned most of the time. Wondering if I was wrong in letting him kiss me passionately as he had, and me for wanting more from him. When will I ever find out what was with it between Molly and him? I was feeling a tug at my heart when I thought of that, and needed to know answers, I needed to understand why I was having these feelings. One minute happy, and the next minute suspicious of everything, and everyone. I didn't want to become a bitter fool, or have my own pity party, but that was what was happening right now.

~

I went to work at the boutique like normal trying to keep my thoughts at bay to get through the day. I didn't want to explain anything to anyone what was going through my mind, but it was confusing to me. Then Aaron has to walk in, of all days, and my heart almost flipped out of my chest at just seeing him. He was heavy in thought, and I knew it must either be about me, or it was about Diana.

Molly called me to her office over the intercom, and it was a sickening feeling I instantly felt, as if I was going to the principal's office to receive some sort of punishment. I couldn't help but think I had done something wrong to either Molly, Aaron, or Carrie Ann. My knees started shaking, and I didn't think I would make it to her office. I sucked in my breath, and knocked on the door letting them know I was coming in before opening the door.

I could see Molly had been crying, and the look on Aaron's face put shivers down my spine. I was scared to death to breath, but some how managed to. There was some serious problems happening, and somehow I was involved.

Molly looked at me asking me to sit in the wing back chair across from her desk, and next to Aaron. The silence was horrible before Molly dabbed her eyes, and cleared her throat to speak. She told me she was trying to be as diplomatic as possible, and fair to me. I groaned, I was being fired. It was all I could do to keep from bursting into tears myself. Molly didn't need to say anymore, I just knew it. I wanted to run and run as far, and as fast as I could right then and there.

As I felt the need to leave as quickly as possible. Aaron reached over for my hand, which I pulled away shaking, and my eyes filling with tears. Tears I was determined I would not let them see. If I was getting fired, I didn't want his sympathy, and definitely not him touching me. I wanted out of the office and yet, I hadn't been told anything yet.

Everything from my past started to flash before me growing up where I didn't have anyone covering my back, and also knowing I wasn't wanted from my birth on. I knew I wasn't going to handle this well. I wanted to escape the office, and escape now.

Molly stood up coming over to sit by me. She took my hands. I was shaking from head to toe, and knew she could feel it as well. She smiled trying to ease my fears, but it wasn't working. I felt my heart beating like drums in my ears, and it was getting hard for me to breathe.

Finally, Molly started talking. It was about Diana. Diana, not me. Aaron pitched in as much as he could get in, between Molly's words. They were talking so fast at the same time I couldn't make heads, or tails what they were saying. I finally stood up, and they stopped. I told them I needed one person at a time to talk to me.

Aaron was the first to speak, saying Diana was making waves on his ability to keep Carrie Ann for the summer. The judge told him he had to make some stipulations, and if Aaron couldn't adjust to what Diana was demanding, Diana was going to keep Carrie Ann for the summer herself. Aaron would only get weekends. Aaron always had her for the summer months while Diana had her for the weekends, but she was playing a game with Aaron's feelings, planning to hurt him as much as possible.

Between the two of them talking, I gathered Diana wants Aaron to hire a full time nanny, so to speak, so Carrie Ann will have consent supervision. If Aaron can't hire someone, Diana will be able to have Carrie Ann for the summer months.

Aaron was at a loss since it was dumped in to his lap just an hour ago. Molly was upset again, because she thinks the world of Carrie Ann, and started crying. It almost brought me to tears seeing her so upset. They were willing to share, but Diana was being spiteful wanting to be sure everyone knew, she was the one in control of everything.

Aaron took my hand again, and this time I let him hold my hand, as he explained a thought he had. After he talked it over with Molly, she agreed it was the best for Carrie Ann.

Molly spoke then telling me they both have seen how much Carrie Ann loves being with me, and how I have been to her as well, teaching her new things, and just seeing to her well being.

Aaron wants me to quit working for Molly, and work for him, so he won't lose Carrie Ann. He was devastated, and at wits end on what else to do. Aaron even offered me a raise, and Molly said the days when I wouldn't be needed at the mansion, I could come back to the boutique without a problem, if I wanted.

Molly didn't want to lose me working for her, but she also wanted what was best for Carrie Ann and for Aaron, as well. I didn't want them to lose Carrie Ann either, and said I would think about it, agreeing to let them know by the end of the day. I wanted to sort some things out in my head, and heart, before I committed to either way. I was at a loss of what I should do.

Molly gave me a huge hug telling me to take my time, and walked out the door dabbing at her eyes leaving Aaron alone in the room with me. I looked at Aaron, and saw the despair in his eyes. He hugged me tenderly kissing my cheek, and asked if there were any questions I needed answered. I told him to come by my place that night, and I would have questions, along my answer if I'll work for him. I left the office letting out a huge sigh of relief, and sucked in a deep breath to finish out the day not seeing either one them.

The other employees wanted to know what had happened, and I didn't know what to say other than I had a big decision to make about leaving the boutique. One of the gals had said that her brother is a friend, of a friend, of Aaron's, as well as Diana, and relayed that his friend thinks Aaron has a new girlfriend, because his demeanor had changed making him happier about something. Also, that Diana wasn't pleased with it either, and going to make Aaron out to be a unfit father by suggesting he was having women over all the time in front of Carrie Ann. I was stunned with that information, but didn't let on anything. I passed it off as silly gossip, but I think in my heart I knew what was going on, and I thought how horrible it was of Diana to do something so conniving, and so despicable.

Once I got home, I took out a pad of paper listing the pros and cons of working for Aaron, as well as a few questions I needed answers to. Maybe some of the questions were none of my business, but I wanted to know, and I wanted everything up front and open, if I was going to give up my job that I loved so much, to go work for him.

Before I realized, my list was filled mostly on the pro side of working for Aaron with other thoughts going on the list. It was a win-win for me, if I could pull it off. Aaron mentioned I would need lesson plans and scheduled activities I would be doing with Carrie Ann during the week, if I took the job, for the judge to review next week. That was when it would be decided in court if Carrie Ann was going to be able to stay with Aaron, or not. How sad she had to be a pawn played in Diane's game.

I had plenty of ideas, but needed a time frame for the other activities Carrie Ann would be involved in with other instructors, like swimming lessons, riding lessons, and any others activities that Diana could throw into the plans. Molly assured me she had a friend that would guide me in the lesson plans, and activities, so I was okay for that part.

When Aaron came over, I went through each and every question I had, which Aaron was more than willing to answer. Also, added a few ideas himself that were terrific, and I made notes on my pad of paper. When he asked if there was anything else, I held up two fingers, and then changed it to three.

Aaron's eyes grew large as I told him the gossip I had heard at the boutique, and wondered if there was any truth to any of it. He smiled and nodded yes telling me since he had seen me that first day in the boutique he started to regain confidence in himself for the first time since his divorce. I paused with that information, and with a sly grin I wanted to know what he thought we should do about the situation.

He didn't want to fuel anything for Diana to use against him, or anymore gossip spread. I would arrive and leave on my scheduled time, and if there were friends over, we agreed to keep our relationship out of the equation during the day.

He would refer to me as Miss Watson, and I would refer to him as Mr. Malone. I could handle that, be professional.

Aaron had no intention to letting me stand aside for the whole summer. He wanted to see me, and see me more often that what we had been. Our nightly talks were lasting into the early hours of the morning. I enjoyed talking with him very much. We decided when we go out together, we would go to places that we wouldn't run into anyone that could report back to Diana. A sad way to work on a relationship, but it would have to do for now.

My second question was answered in the first, and the third question wasn't much of a question. I had something I needed to tell him, but not sure how so I leaned over whispering in his ear that it was something that might scare him off. He shook his head no, nothing could scare him off when it came to me. I continued my short confession that I was falling in love with him.

No response from him made me panic. I slowly pulled away just as he grabbed me by my shoulders telling me there was no way news like that could ever scare him away, and with that he brought his lips to mine kissing me the most tender kiss of all. I could have melted right then in his arms.

His smile warmed my heart, and I could feel the static we were creating grow strong. He slowly got up asking me if I had come to my answer on working for him, and I shook my head yes. We ended that with more kisses before he left that night.

CHAPTER 8

After Aaron met with Diana to get the lessons with times, and dates for the summer activities she wanted Carrie Ann to participate in, I met with Molly's friend, Renee, that was a second grade teacher in Jasper. Her help was tremendously insightful to where I was able to pull together three months of other activities, lunch, and field trips I planned for Carrie Ann. I filled in the schedule completely within two days. I don't think I would have done as well if it hadn't been for Renee.

I showed Aaron and Molly what I had scheduled, which they were very impressed, even though they weren't the ones we had to impress. Diana had the final say in everything, including the instructors for swimming, horseback riding, tennis, and dancing lessons. We were lucky enough she had provided their names and telephone numbers whether it was on purpose, or accidental, it didn't matter.

The day before Aaron had to meet with the judge and Diana, he was informed that I would have to go with him. Diana wanted to be sure I would be suitable to care for her daughter. What a slap in the face that was to me, but I had to let it slide not taking it personally. Knowing what I learned about Diana's rearing of Carrie Ann, she had no room to judge me by far.

I was at a loss on what I should say, not say, what to wear, or not wear, for that meeting. Molly had everything under control for me, by helping me pick a suitable outfit.

On the drive to the court house Aaron said that if they ask if I have prior experience, inform them I was in college to become a teacher. I didn't have to tell them what area of teaching I was planning, unless they asked. I didn't need to give them more information than what they asked.

I was a nervous wreck by the time we were called into the judge's chamber to discuss everything. My stomach was in tight knots, and growling from not eating any breakfast, I was sure. The judge asked very few questions of me to answer, but it was good that Aaron had prepped me on my education goals of becoming a teacher, because that was the very first question I needed to answer. I also presented my schedule of plans to the judge, which he looked over carefully nodding his head as he read everything.

After a half hour the judge decided after everything was looked over several times, that he couldn't see any reason why Aaron wouldn't be allowed to have Carrie Ann for the summer. Aaron had done everything that Diana demanded, and in a record time.

Diana was furious, and made the judge hesitate before he said she would get Carrie Ann on the weekends, and weekends only. Diana would have to pick Carrie Ann up at four PM on Friday nights, and promptly return her to Aaron's house no later that six PM on Sunday night. If she breaches that agreement, she wouldn't be allowed to have her only every other weekends.

The judge told everyone that there should be no reason to play the child as a pawn like in a chess game, as it tends to be the game he is seeing being played out by Diana. It was only hurting the child, as well as the other parent involved, in her scheme. He said it had to stop, and better stop now. Banged the gavel, and we were excused

Diana's attorney advised her to take the deal. Be happy for the weekends which she hesitated, but finally agreed. Once that was signed, we were free to leave.

Aaron immediately thanked me for all the work I had done on the plans, for being at the courthouse with him to answer questions, and for the summer I was about to begin in a week. He announced we were going out to lunch to celebrate our victory against Diana. I was starved, and couldn't wait to cat something.

It was a nice secluded restaurant among the many juniper trees a little out of town in the country. It was very charming with delicious homemade meals to choose from.

Aaron and I had plenty of time to talk, and go over my lesson plans once again. He wanted to be sure I had a chance to purchase items I would need to get started giving me a credit card to use when I went to the teaching store, where Renee said I could get about everything I could possibly need to start with. I accepted the card graciously, as I knew I would need supplies.

Aaron was looking over the paperwork when he told me

every instructor Diana hired were friends, or family of hers, in one way or another. I would have to deal with the possible and probable sarcasm from them, but not to let it bother me. They would be doing it to hurt him, not me. That was good to know in advance.

After we were at Aaron's home, he suggested we go for a swim after dinner about nine o'clock if possible. Even though it was only June the days were hot and humid already. I could use a refresher after today's ordeal as well.

〜

Everything went very well the first couple of weeks at Aaron's with the lesson plans. The schedules were pretty much in place for everyone to follow, and I was quite surprised how easy my days seemed to flow. We could see the happiness in Carrie Ann.

That was until that one Thursday later in the morning. Carrie Ann's swim instructor was ten minutes late to her lesson, once again. It was starting to become a habit of hers. Carrie Ann, and I patiently waited for her at the pool. I learned right from the start that she was Diana's half sister, Janet, and in her eyes, Diana could do no wrong stating Aaron was being an ass to Diana. I made sure to ignore the snide comments Janet rendered while in her presence, but kept them in the back of my head until later when I wrote them in my journal.

One thing I did ask of her was not to talk ill of Aaron in front of Carrie Ann, and she just looked at me like I had asked her for a million dollars, rolled her eyes while she walked away. I didn't care, she had no right to do it in front of Carrie Ann.

On her first day there, she made a point to let me know that my being there was not what she wanted, and I was to excuse myself at that time to leave her alone with Carrie Ann, which I complied. I usually went into the kitchen, and sat at the counter with a glass of iced tea, while I chatted with Mary. Mary would be busy in the kitchen preparing the meals, but never too busy to chat as she worked. She was so kind, and easy to talk with, just like her twin Molly.

Carrie Ann would follow Janet into the house after the lessons were over, and where Janet would collect her envelope containing her pay. Aaron should deduct her pay on the days she's late, but that wasn't my business. However, on that day Janet was late to start the swim lessons, and when she came into the kitchen for the envelope with her pay, she was also ten minutes early, but most importantly, Carrie Ann wasn't with her.

Immediately, I asked where Carrie Ann was. Janet said she was sitting on the pool steps waiting for me. I jumped off the stool running out the door yelling to Mary to get Mr. Malone out back quickly.

As I went through the pool gate, the horror I saw took my breath away. Carrie Ann was in the middle of the pool flaying her arms about trying to stay above the water making more splashes than anything, while gulping for air. I was in the pool, and reached her just as she slipped under water. When I grabbed her bringing her to the top, she was hanging onto me with a death grip, that I actually had to struggle to get to the side of the pool myself. The poor child was so scared shaking like a leaf, and coughing up water with every breath she took.

Aaron was there by then, and dear Janet was standing

by the pool just watching with her arms folded across her chest in disgust. Everyone had come to the pool. I noticed Molly had made it over from the store as well. Mary must have called her immediately after calling Aaron, and 911. Carrie Ann was crying hard not letting her grip go of me. Not even for Aaron. I heard sirens in the distance, and knew Carrie Ann was going to get medical help soon. Carrie Ann had a death grip around my neck making it a challenge for me to breathe. Aaron helped us out of the pool and over to the bench, so I could sit down with Carrie Ann on my lap.

The paramedics wanted to take Carrie Ann, so they could check her out, but she remained with her death grip to me. I sat on the gurney they had out to transport her to the hospital, holding Carrie Ann, trying to talk to her. So many people were talking at once making Carrie Ann scared of everyone, with everything that had happened, and what was going on around her now.

I finally was able to get her to let the paramedic listen to her heart by showing her it wouldn't hurt by letting them do mine first. It was only then she allowed them to look her over, but remained on my lap. Once they were done, and ready to transport her to the hospital, she grabbed back onto me in that same grip. Poor child was so frightened.

They allowed me to hold her as they transported us to the hospital. Aaron sitting next to me trying to help in every way he could. Carrie Ann wasn't having anything to do with anyone, but me. I felt bad for Aaron, but every time I tried to get Carrie Ann to go to him, she gripped me even tighter. Finally, after two hours at the hospital, she went to her dad. I quietly excused myself from them.

I didn't take more than two or three steps away from them

when I felt faint, and down I went. I was drained from the emotional day. When I woke up, I was in the cubicle next to Carrie Ann with oxygen on my face. I told everyone I was fine, just wanted to go home, and was released from the hospital. It was embarrassing for me to faint like that, but Aaron didn't think anything bad of it. He was splitting his time between me, and Carrie Ann which, I didn't feel was necessary. Carrie Ann needed him, and I was fine. Aaron had his driver take me home in semi-wet clothes and all.

I made my way to my bathroom to shower, and put my pajamas on. I was so shaken by everything that had happened. I was also so furious at Janet for leaving a child alone in the pool. You just don't do that with children, and she was a so-called professional swim instructor. Where was her brain? How irresponsible on her part. I kept seeing the way she stood, watching everything take place, without assisting. That really bothered me. I don't know when she left the area, but I bet she didn't even have any remorse for what could have happened to Carrie Ann.

It wasn't until after ten that night when Aaron came to my door. I had been waiting for some kind of news, but dozed off on the couch, hoping someone would let me know something, anything on Carrie Ann. Aaron hugged me thanking me over, and over, for saving Carrie Ann's life. My quick thinking, and fast acting upon an emergency as I had done, could never be repaid. All he needed to know was that his daughter was going to be alright, and a precious life had been saved.

I hung onto him as he talked to me, shaking every second. I was so happy to hear Carrie Ann was going to be alright, and more than happy to help when she needed me. Aaron didn't stay much longer, as he was going back to spend the night at the hospital with his daughter. Molly was with her now while Carrie Ann was sleeping, but not soundly. Diana doesn't like hospitals, so she went home once she saw Carrie Ann was going to be fine. Wow! What a concerned mother Diana wasn't! Aaron thank me once again, and to let me know he was holding a meeting the next day. It was necessary for me to be there.

～

Carrie Ann was released the next afternoon, and Aaron brought her home. She was in her bedroom tucked in her bed resting, like the doctor instructed for the next few days. Mary was with her for the time being, while Aaron held the meeting with all the instructors hired for Carrie Ann.

He didn't look very happy. You could tell he was tired himself, with the dark circles around his eyes, and his hair not combed his normal way. Everyone came in the office. Janet came up to me saying she thought maybe she owed me a thank you for saving Carrie Ann. I was still angry with her, and shook my head as I rolled my eyes, as I told her to get away from me between my clenched teeth. She looked stunned at first, but then got this grin on her face, as if she done nothing wrong. She didn't owe me nothing, she owed Aaron and Carrie Ann an apology big time, but I am sure she'll never utter anything to them.

Aaron began by thanking everyone for coming in, and started into his reason for the meeting. He explained what had happened yesterday, and how close he came to losing his child, his only child. He said if any of us weren't happy working there, we were free to leave, as his daughter is the most important thing to him. He wasn't going to have anyone who didn't take their job seriously be on his property.

He thanked me once again for my quick action in saving his daughter, and with that, he turned to Janet telling her she was fired. He made it clear she was never allowed to set foot on the property again.

Janet looked shocked that she was fired, and started to complain. Aaron had her escorted from the room, and off the property. Everyone else wanted to keep their jobs, and hoped they had been doing a good job for him. He was satisfied with their performances, and was glad they stayed.

He left the room as the others came over to thank me for saving Carrie Ann. They seemed genuinely honest, and soon left. I didn't know what I was to do, so when Mary came downstairs, I asked if there was anything instructed for me. Aaron had gone to Carrie Ann's room where he laid down next to her, and finally fell asleep, so she thought I might just go home and rest myself. She hugged, and thanked me with tears in her eyes before I left.

I needed to get some rest myself, so I didn't argue with Mary's suggestion. The walk back to my house seemed as if it took days for me to reach my place. I had so many thoughts rushing through my mind trying to make sense of Janet, and her lack of compassion, lack of concern, lack of responsibility, and lack of life in general. She surely will have to answer later in life.

Once I reached my home, I opened the door, and quickly went inside to get some rest. I ended up sleeping through the rest of the day and night at well. I didn't get a call from Aaron during the night, which I could understand. He was where he needed to be, and he was getting some well deserved sleep himself.

When I woke up, I was in a daze thinking it had to have been a bad dream with everything that had happened yesterday, but I knew it wasn't, and began to cry. I cried at how close Aaron had been to losing his precious daughter, cried that it was something that should have never happened, and cried from the fear of all the "what if's" that flooded my thoughts right then. It took me all this time to grasp everything, and it hit me hard then.

I opened my door to find another vase filled with all these beautiful flowers on my little porch from Aaron. He wrote me the kindest note thanking me once again, and was giving me the day off. He asked if I could drop by later to see Carrie Ann and him, by having lunch with them.

I breathed in a large sigh, holding the note to my chest, and smiled as I brought the vase in setting it on the table. I was going to be okay, and knew what I had done would never be forgotten by Aaron, or anyone else, myself included.

CHAPTER 9

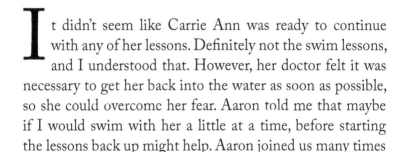

It didn't seem like Carrie Ann was ready to continue with any of her lessons. Definitely not the swim lessons, and I understood that. However, her doctor felt it was necessary to get her back into the water as soon as possible, so she could overcome her fear. Aaron told me that maybe if I would swim with her a little at a time, before starting the lessons back up might help. Aaron joined us many times as Carrie Ann and I sat on the bench by the pool watching him.

I was able to get Carrie Ann to sit with me on the bench next to the pool more and more as the week went by, and we talked about how important it was for her to get back in the pool, to take lessons to become a strong swimmer, so nothing like that ever happens to her again.

She started to cry saying she was too scared, so I told her something that had happened to me when I was only six years old. Only I wasn't taking lessons, and didn't have any idea what to do. The family I was living with at that time had a son that had a bully streak in him, and he threw me in the pool through all my protests. That got Carrie Ann's attention.

I was scared too, very scared, and if his older sister hadn't pulled me out, I probably wouldn't be here telling her that now. I didn't want to ever be near any body of water again, and even refused to take my baths because of the fear I had. I stayed clear of the boy until I was placed in another foster home, because he was such a bully.

The YMCA offered free swimming lessons, and my social worker encouraged my new foster parents to sign me up, which they did. I sat on the side of the pool for several classes until the swim instructor coaxed me into the pool with her. I didn't want to go in the water, but she was very nice to me, and thought if I trusted her maybe I would actually learn to swim. It took awhile. I hung onto her with every ounce of strength in me, because I was plagued with the fear of that day. Now, I can swim pretty good, and good enough to help a special little girl when she needed me the most, just the other week, as I touched her little nose with my finger. I could see in her eyes things were clicking, and she asked if I would help her get over her fear, and be with her during her lessons.

Once I agreed, she asked if we could sit on the steps of the pool in the water, and we did. Slowly, she allowed me to take her out a little more from the step, as she hung onto my hands. When Aaron was there, he was at a loss for words, but he knew if anyone could get through to Carrie Ann, it would be me.

Aaron and Molly were watching through the French doors of Aaron's office, and I knew from the smile on their faces, they were happy with the progress I had already made. Carrie Ann looked up at them, waved, and she was smiling. I will stay with her during her swim lessons as long as she feels she needs me. I vowed I wouldn't let it happen to her again, to her as well as to myself. It scared me to the core that day, and I knew Aaron was scared as well.

The family reunion was going to be held soon, and I never knew how much they put into making it a success. They not only had tons of food, but small booths were set up for the kids to play, and win prizes. Music could be heard all the way to my place, as car load after car load of family pulled in. The alley/driveway was bumper to bumper vehicles, and my passage through the bushes was blocked. I didn't mind, I didn't need to get through it today.

Aaron made a point of personally inviting me, even though I'm not family, and provided me with their reunion tee shirt. I only knew a handful of people, but everyone seemed very friendly, and talked to me as if I was part of the family.

To kick the fun off, Aaron welcomed everyone, by making introductions of the newest members to the family. He also made everyone welcome me telling them I was also family, and I had saved his little girl from drowning last month. They all cheered, and congratulated me throughout the day and night.

I felt like I was part of the family that day, and enjoyed it very much. Everything with Aaron, and me, were going along very nicely. Still under the radar with our relationship, and that made me feel absolutely great. Aaron has yet to tell me he loves me, but I guess when he does all the things he does for me, even though he doesn't have to. I would like to have him utter those three little words sometime though. I think it would validate what we have together.

We would have movie night on the weekends Carrie Ann was gone. We made it to the drive-in a few times, but mostly we watched the movie at my place, or his. Depending on what was going on at the time. I would pull the couch out to make a bed where we would snuggle up together while eating popcorn, as we watched the movie.

Everything was going smoothly, and Carrie Ann was back to being her bubbly self once again. Aaron took the field trips with us, which made it extra special for Carrie Ann. We had several places we went, but the butterfly farm seemed to be Carrie Ann's favorite. We had studied the butterflies for two weeks beforehand, and released our own painted lady butterflies we had ordered in the larva stage to grow at the house. It was amazing how much Carrie Ann enjoyed what she was learning.

While on that field trip she had taken the part of teacher explaining every step of the process to her dad. He played along asking her question after question on everything. It was so nice to see them interact with each other on the topics.

I was sad that the summer was almost over, and Carrie Ann would be leaving to go back with her mom. I would probably go back to working at the boutique the same time. I had been taking my college classes all summer long at night. Most of them I tested out of to hurry the process faster. I was almost through with my Associates degree, and was ready to continue on to my Bachelor degree. I changed my goal deciding I wanted to become a research librarian.

Our last outing together was to the county fair before Carrie Ann had to leave for her mom's. We made sure we enjoyed ourselves, by going on many rides, eating the best foods, and playing several games, which Carrie Ann ended up winning a few stuffed animals. She was having a great time, until we had to leave. She didn't want to go to her mom's, she wanted to stay with Aaron. I stepped back, as he needed to talk to her about what the court said, and how she was so important to him, but it had to be that way, assuring her she would be back Friday nights for the weekend. We could do something fun then, and finally she agreed, as long as I could be there, too. Aaron agreed wholeheartedly to that stipulation without a second thought.

We started having some furious thunderstorms lately, and making it home after class had been a struggle at times, until Aaron started picking me up at college to drive me home. I don't know what else he can do to help me as he does, but he is amazing.

Many nights after I would be in bed he'd call just to tell me good night, and we'd end up talking for over an hour or two sometimes. I don't know where we find things to talk about, but we always do. I fall asleep knowing he does have feelings for me.

It was one night he was having his friends over to watch a football game that I knew not to bother him. We hadn't figured out which friend was the one spilling their guts out to get back to Diana, but we didn't want to add fuel to the situation.

I was laying in bed reading, when I heard the thunder start rumbling loud, with long lightning bolts lighting up the sky.

It was going to be one of those storms that I knew I wasn't going to like. I heard this creaking noise that got louder and louder, and before I realized it was the tree in Miss Nelson's backyard coming through my house. Suddenly everything went black on me.

I knew I wasn't in my bed, but I couldn't open my eyes for some reason. My legs and head were hurting so much, but I had no strength in me for anything. My body ached, as if I had run a marathon, and hadn't stopped running yet. I had a hard time trying to breathe, even the slightest breath I would take. I didn't like this feeling at all. I could hear people talking around me. At first, I couldn't make out what they were saying, but I recognized Molly, Mary, and Aaron's voices. Their words weren't making any sense to me though. What was going on??

I tried to talk, but there was so much noise next to my head it was impossible to know if they could hear me. Then, everything would go black again. I don't know for how long I was asleep, but I decided I had to fight the pain, and quit going back to the blackness I kept experiencing.

One night I heard Molly and Aaron talking. I could hear Aaron telling her that he loved me so much, and he couldn't bare to lose me. Molly asked if he has told me that himself, telling him he needed to tell me how he felt. It might help me come out of it, whatever that was, I thought to myself. Then it was black again.

I was able to think, but that was it. I felt the overwhelming love for Aaron, and couldn't do anything about it until I could open my eyes, but they just refused to open. I felt I was going to lose Aaron if I didn't try hard. I tried to focus on it every chance I could, but nothing worked.

One time I felt Aaron holding my hand. That was a good start, I could feel something now, just needed to get my eyes to open, or my body to move…. something… anything.

Aaron was whispering in my ear telling me how much he loved me, and how he wanted me to get better soon. I had a hold on his heart that was aching without me there. His words were so kind and loving, and I wanted to reach out to him more than ever. I wanted him to know how much I loved him as well. What has happened to me? Was I going to die, and just lingering around until I was taken? I wanted to shout "help me" but why couldn't I?

I felt the side of my face get wet. I knew they were Aaron's tears. Open eyes, open!!! He kissed me, and I couldn't even respond. I knew when he went home that night, as it got very quiet, and I felt very alone.

Later the next morning, I think I made a movement when the nurse was there. My eyes fluttered, and I was able to finally open them. I grabbed the nurse by her hand, and she smiled calling out for the doctor who rushed in.

He was smiling as well when he saw me, and welcomed me back to being awake. I learned four days had passed as I laid there in that room. They called Aaron, but he was at a meeting, so they called Molly to come over. Everyone was so happy for me. I asked to get cleaned up. The nurse said as soon as she could, she would be back to help me.

In the meantime, Molly came running into my room so excited to see me, with tears in her eyes she hugged, and kissed my cheeks over and over. I asked her what had happened, and why was I there.

She explained that Miss Nelson's tree uprooted during the storm crashing over the cottage, pinning me in bed.

Aaron's friend, Danny, tried to drive down the alley to get to the house to watch the game with the guys, when he saw the commotion going on. The fire department was there using chain saws to cut the tree, and paramedics on stand by to make sure no one was under all the rubble. Police were blocking off the road to cars, and assisting where ever they needed.

When Danny finally made it to the house, he told Aaron about Miss Nelson's tree in her backyard had uprooted stating it smashed that little house behind Jonathan's large house flat to the ground. Aaron jumped to his feet, and ran all the way to your house. They weren't going to allow him in the area, but he put up such a fuss, they finally gave in. Aaron used his bare hands to dig things out, and throw boards to the side until he found me pinned under the tree. He uncovered me, and scooped me in his arms carrying me to the paramedics waiting. I was unconscious and bleeding all over.

Aaron stayed with me in the ambulance to the hospital, and for two days straight, by my bed in the hospital. The doctor said it was a miracle I was even alive with all the weight on me, but I was hanging on, by the grace of God.

They were taking shifts being with me, so I wouldn't be alone if I were to wake up. Aaron still wouldn't leave, and would get some sleep in my room, by sleeping in a recliner. Mary and Molly brought him meals, and fresh clothes daily, but he hardly touched the food, and didn't change his clothes. He said the blood on his clothes was a reminder of what had happened to me, and until I was better, he wouldn't change. Molly finally put her foot down, so he went home to shower, and he changed then.

He had to leave to clean up, because he had to go see his attorney friend today, but will be back in the afternoon. I told Molly I wanted to get cleaned up quickly with a bath, and I could wash my hair. I had to be helped with everything, as painful as it was for me, but we managed to get it done before Aaron came in.

Aaron walked in the room, looked at Molly, then to me, and burst into tears of happiness. Molly waved goodbye, and left Aaron alone with me. He scooped me into his arms holding me close, telling me how happy he was all the while planting kisses on me. I was still very weak and in pain, but I hugged him with all I had.

I was never so happy to open my eyes that morning, and having Aaron right there with me right now, holding me in his arms. He gently rocked me back and forth telling me he was so worried he lost me, and finally, finally told me he was in love with me. I told him that made me the happiest of all. I loved him as well.

Aaron stayed until the doctor came by to see me. The doctor wanted me to stay for another day or so, of observation to be on the safe side, before he would release me. Aaron said he would be back early in the morning, and be with me until I could go home.

Home? I didn't have a home to go to anymore. I didn't have anything left. My clothes were ruined, my personal belongings were destroyed, nothing but nothing that belonged to me was salvaged in the mess.

I cried myself to sleep that night. I felt like I did when going from one foster home to another with nothing, for the first time since arriving in Jasper. How was I going to go on from here when all I had was a pair of pajamas to my name?

CHAPTER 10

The next morning when I woke up, I was feeling so depressed. The nurse asked why I was so sad, and I told her I had lost everything with that tree destroying where I lived, and didn't have a place to live any longer. No home, no clothes, no nothing period. She said there was always a silver lining in every dark cloud, and not to let it get me down. She felt sure something good was going to happen for me.

I had just finished breakfast, what little I ate, when Aaron came through my door with shopping bags after shopping bags in his arms. He had gone shopping for me as a get-well-glad-your-better gifts, as he called them. I started crying, and he set the bags down coming on the bed to hold me.

I blubbered out what I had felt last night, and all through the night, about losing everything between my tears and gulps of breathing, which was still very painful to do. Even how I had felt like I was going to another foster home, as I had as a kid growing up. I was shaking and crying so hard, I didn't know what else to do, but cling to him. I was at a loss not knowing what I was going to do.

He pulled away from me while holding my shoulders saying I had absolutely nothing to worry about, with the smile I had grown to love. He told I didn't have to worry, I would be going to his house. Mary, Molly, and the staff, have been busy getting the guest room downstairs ready for me, and everyone is so excited for me to come. They had everything ready, and he wasn't going to take no for an answer.

I calmed down drying my eyes telling him I couldn't do that to him, or them. It was very generous, but I didn't know what to do. He told me I had helped him out with something he could never pay me back for this past summer, and it was something he felt he could help me with. He also told me he, Molly, and Mary, went through the rubble of my home. They were able to retrieve a few of my personal items. I asked about my journal, and he confirmed they found it. They had it all in a box waiting for me to go through at his house.

I agreed to go stay at his house, but he wouldn't have to wait on me, I planned to get back to work as soon as I could at the boutique, and earn my stay there. He reached for me holding my face in his hands telling me he loved me, and kissed me letting me know he truly understood.

The doctor stepped in clearing his throat, and smiled. He was glad I was feeling better, as he took my vitals, he informed me he was setting me up with a physical therapist that would come in daily, until I gained the strength back in my legs and arms, and a visiting nurse that would come weekly, whenever I was going to be released.

He was going to release me in a few more days if I had made some improvement. I shook my head stating that I planned on that, and Aaron shook the doctors hand thanking him for everything he had done for me.

I was excited to be leaving in a few days. Aaron handed me the bags he brought in saying he had to guess on the sizes, so he hoped everything fit, and I liked them. He was spot on with the sizes, even down to the fancy lingerie. He actually went in the store himself to pick everything out. He spared no expense with the purchases either.

Molly came back in the door after knocking, and was happy to hear the news as well. She informed us that everything at the house was ready for me, whenever I was released, and the entire staff were pleased to learn that I would be staying there.

～

Before I was released I had to go through a few more tests. The swelling in my head had gone done immensely, which was the biggest concern they had with that tree pinning me down the way it had. My arms and legs were still extremely weak yet, and a dark shade of purple, but physical therapy was working wonders with me gaining my strength. The bruises would go away in time. I was exhausted after the workout, and winced several times from the pain, but they assured me it would help. That was my goal, to be better, and on my own walking accord.

The day finally arrived when I would be released. I couldn't be more happier than I was. They had been very nice to me in the hospital, so that wasn't an issue. Just the whole atmosphere of being so confined was bothering me.

The nurse helped me dressed while Aaron waited outside the curtain. That took longer than normal because I didn't have the co-operation of my limbs like I thought I had. I was ready to cry, and it showed on my face. The nurse assured me that I would have to take things very slow for awhile. The damage to my nerves was extensive, but in time I should have regain full use at what it was before the tree fell on me.

Ready to go, and the nurse brought in the wheelchair to transport me to Aaron's car waiting for me outside the emergency room doors. Everyone said their good-byes to me as I was rolled towards those doors. The sun hit my face, and it felt so good feeling the warmth, and smelling the fresh air. Never thought I had missed it, but I had.

Aaron made sure to drive through the front gate, so I wouldn't see what was left of my little place. It was all rubble piled up to be removed. I was thankful I didn't have to see it to remind me what had happened. Bad enough my arms and legs reminded me of it every single day.

Everyone at the house had come outside to greet me when we pulled in, and when Aaron lifted me into the wheelchair, they all cheered. They were lined up along the sidewalk to the door. Hanging on the door was a huge "Welcome Home Abby" sign.

Once inside the house, there were gifts and cake on the dining room table for me. I was overwhelmed with their thoughtfulness and kindness. Carrie Ann was there helping serve the cake, but keeping her distance from me. That concerned me. I must really have scared her with the bruising on my face, arms, and legs. The cuts were pretty deep, and stitched closed, but it was enough to keep her at bay.

After everyone ate their cake, they handed me their gifts to open. Shortly they went back to work. Carrie Ann stood at the opposite end of the table staring at me. I smiled at her, and asked her to help me with the gifts. She hesitated, but slowly came over where she burst into tears.

I hugged her asking what was wrong. All I could get between her heavy sobs was that she was so sorry I couldn't walk anymore, and the tree fell, and she thought I had died, and so did her daddy, and he was sad, and everyone was crying in the house, and she just got scared she'd never see me again.

I shushed her telling her I was going to be fine. I was scared too, but with the help of everyone, I will be strong again. I will walk again because I was going to work hard at it. I thanked her for the pictures she drew while I was in the hospital, and thought they were beautiful. She stopped crying, and asked if she could help me learn to walk again, like I had helped her learn how to swim again. I smiled and told her she sure could. I could use all the help, especially from her.

She smiled saying she would help me every day possible. I looked up, and saw Aaron standing at the door wiping his eyes. He smiled before he walked in saying I needed to get some rest, and if Carrie Ann could carry everything into my room, that would be a great help. She was eager to gather everything up, and follow Aaron pushing me in a wheelchair into the bedroom.

The staff had the bedroom arranged perfect for me. I had the room off the kitchen so when I couldn't get up, Mary would be able to hear me, and come help. Aaron moved into the bedroom next to mine with a pocket door between us, and Carrie Ann moved in the room across the hall, so she wouldn't be upstairs by herself.

Aaron lifted me up from the wheelchair, and gently put me down on the bed. Carrie Ann fluffed the pillows behind my head, and asked if she could climb on the bed next to me. I told her she sure could. Very carefully up she came, and asked if she could snuggle up next to me too.

Aaron left us there, and went to his office. Carrie Ann asked if my legs and arms hurt to touch. I explained everything to her at a level she would understand. Once she was satisfied, she closed her eyes, and fell asleep snuggled against me.

It was such a precious moment for me that Carrie Ann was so concerned, and wanted to be close to me as she was. I looked around my room. I felt the warmth and love that was placed in there to make me comfortable. This family was truly a beautiful family inside, and out.

I dozed off myself. When I opened my eyes, Carrie Ann was gone, and Aaron was resting in the chair next to me. He smiled asking if he could sit on the bed next to me. I patted a spot for him, and asked where Carrie Ann was. Diana had picked her up. Aaron didn't think it would be a good idea for Diana to see Carrie Ann curled up next to me, so he moved her before Diana came in. Probably a good idea. Aaron didn't need to explain my presence being there to her. Aaron was sure Carrie Ann would tell Diana everything she could, and Diana would squeeze every bit of information out of her.

Aaron told me he had an attorney friend, Eric, that was

going to handle my lawsuit against Miss Nelson's insurance company, if I didn't mind. Aaron explained everything that had happened, and that Miss Nelson had been advised several times, she needed to attend to that tree before someone got hurt, but she hadn't done anything, and now someone was hurt, me. I suffered a serious injury at that, and hopefully not permanent. I didn't know anything about what was legal, or what wasn't, and I trusted Aaron, so I agreed.

Aaron and I talked for hours that night. I told him I thought I could hear him when he found me under the mess. He asked what I thought I had heard, and I told him, "Don't worry, I've got you babe" and "Don't leave me babe". Aaron smiled saying he was so glad I heard him, because those were the words he did say to me. He didn't want to lose me, and I looked so terribly hurt he thought he would, and he didn't think he could handle it. I hugged him thanking him for finding me, and helping me with everything.

Aaron had carried my limp body to the ambulance waiting, and went to the hospital in the ambulance with me. He held my hand the entire way there, until the doctor and nurse had him leave, so they could tend to me. The doctor had told Aaron I had a fifty-fifty chance of making it through the night, because of the trauma to my back, legs, and head.

When Molly arrived, he told her the prognosis, and they prayed over me. They believe those prayers helped, because by morning I had already made improvement even though I was still unconscious. All through the day Aaron prayed never leaving my side. He would talk softly into my ear, so it wouldn't cause any pain, and they kept the room dimly lit, even though my eyes were swollen shut.

He fell asleep on the bed with me in his arms keeping me safe, and feeling loved. I had the best of the best when it came to Aaron. I may never understand why Diana felt the need to use him, and quite frankly, abuse him, the way she had. Aaron was a gem, and I am the one in his arms now.

～

Weeks passed with daily physical therapy that wasn't as painful as it had been in the beginning. I was getting much better gaining the strength back that I had lost. My attorney, Eric, stopped by on a few occasions to see how I was doing, and to give me updates on the claim we put in to Miss Nelson's insurance company. They, of course, wanted to fight it, but was now coming around to what Eric felt would be a decent settlement, with all the reports and photos he provided.

I asked Eric for a copy of everything, and when I saw the photos of me, of the house, and everything, I was shocked. I looked a horrible mess with blood all over me, bruises that followed, doctor reports, and photos of my house, or what I should say what was the remains of it.

There was one photograph some reporter had taken where Aaron was carrying my limp lifeless body in his arms towards the ambulance. We were both covered in lots of blood, and the look on Aaron's face was so grim, it broke my heart. It shook me up tremendously. I couldn't even imagine what he was feeling at that time. It was printed in the paper as a good "Samaritan" helping with saving my life. There was a long story with the photo, and they put Aaron's name in the story. Just the photograph was enough to make my chest begin to hurt, and my head start to throb. There was nothing left but a pile of rubble. It was too much for me to deal with right then. I asked Eric to get Mary or Aaron because I was having a panic attack, and couldn't shake it off.

Mary and Aaron came running into the room just as I was trying to catch my breath. I was a sight for sorry eyes, I was sure, but I was past caring at that time. I couldn't breathe, and I was scared. The doctor arrived in no time giving me a shot to calm down. Calm me down, it put me to sleep for hours.

When I woke up, Aaron was in the chair next to me holding my hand planting little kisses on my fingertips. Everyone else had left after the doctor gave instructions that I didn't need to see anything for awhile, as it was too much for me to handle at that time. I had been through enough trauma to last me for some time to come. Eric was so upset with himself he couldn't handle it, and left right after the doctor gave me a shot. Aaron told Eric no one knew what would have happened, and he had only done what I had asked of him. Eric asked if he could come by in a few days to apologize to me himself, and Aaron agreed without hesitation.

I asked Mary to bring me some books to read the next day, since I was bedridden, on the founding of Jasper, and the family. I was consumed with everything, and learning more and more about the area, and the family. I tried to imagine how everything was at that time, and the construction of this house. It was then that I started to piece things together on Aaron's family. When I reached the chapter on his grandfather's information it all made sense. I wanted to shout out what I had just learned, but knew I needed to find out more.

Aaron's grandfather was married to Miss Nelson. The same Miss Nelson that had that tree in her backyard that fell on me. The same Miss Nelson that wouldn't have anything to do with her husband. The same woman that was a bitter scorned woman to this day. The same Miss Nelson that his grandfather finally divorced, and later married a younger lady in town, by the name of Molly Masters.

MOLLY!!! Molly was Aaron's grandmother. The grandmother that raised him after his parents were killed in that plane crash. The same crash that took her son, daughter-in-law and Aaron's brother and sister.

I sat back against my pillows shaking my head, everything made sense now. I had the last piece to the puzzle known. But, why did Aaron call her Molly and not grandmother? Maybe I didn't have the entire puzzle figured out after all. Molly's twin sister, Mary, had married Aaron's grandfather's younger brother. Once Mary's husband died, in his sixties to heart failure, she began working at the house for Molly and Anson, the grandfather. I felt like I hit the jackpot reading all that information, and knew why Aaron and Molly seemed so close, and why he included Molly and Mary with all the family ordeals. I needed to talk to Molly and Aaron as soon as I could.

Aaron and Molly both came into my room the next morning, as I had asked. I told them I had read the book on the family, and was wondering if the Molly Masters was the same as Molly Malone standing in the room with me. I saw two sets of eyes grow big, and they told me everything then. The reason Aaron calls Molly by her name, because Molly was worried about the people that came into her store if they knew she was his grandmother. They agreed when

Aaron started getting his books published they'd keep their relationship quiet, mostly for safety factors. Safety for her, for him and for Carrie Ann. I was glad they confessed, and told them the thoughts I had been having, which we all got a laugh from that. Especially when I thought Molly was a cougar!! I was glad they weren't mad, and happy to know, I was the one Aaron was in love with.

The Fall Festival was getting close, and I was determined I was going to do my share for it, which I did. Aaron thought I should just pass on it, but I wouldn't hear of it. Carrie Ann and I will man the fishing booth where I can sit when needed. It was a super easy booth to do, and finally Aaron agreed. Aaron helped me onto the hay wagon for the annual hayride through the neighborhood when the festival was ending. I looked forward to that, and didn't want to be left behind. It was a great event, and everyone had a wonderful time. I actually hated to see it come to an end, but once the fireworks were done people started leaving. It was a long day for everyone. After Mary assisted me on my shower, I was in bed asleep within minutes.

On the hayride was when I saw the space where my little home had once stood.

Everything had been cleared away, and a large garage was in the process of being built in the empty space. It sadden my heart to think I would still be there, and still able to work back down at the boutique, as well as house sitting for Jonathon and Amber. If only Miss Nelson had only taken care of business with that tree when she had been advised. But, I have had to let go of those bad feelings. When I think about it, I am happy where I am right now, and deal with what I have been given, a second chance.

⁓

Thanksgiving was truly a time for me to be thankful this year with what I had been through, and I made it known, as we gave thanks at the table to each and everyone. I may not have a biological family, but I have one large one right there at the table that makes me feel welcomed. How grateful I am.

I am finally able to walk on my own, by taking smaller and slower steps, than in the past. I went shopping at the mall with Molly one afternoon for a few Christmas gifts, and it felt good to be out, away from the house. Molly and I had lunch at that tiny café when we were done, and those cheeseburgers were still as delicious as the first time we were there. I sensed Molly knew I was growing tired, and lunch gave me the needed rest. Now that the cat is out of the bag as to her relationship with Aaron, we have found more things to talk about. Aaron commented that we were like two little birds chirping nonstop!

Aaron was busy overseeing the house being decorated for Christmas, and it was just beautiful already, and only partly done. I was looking forward to Christmas again, and being a part of the planning they do.

Aaron and I went out to dinner many nights since my ability to walk had improved so much. We ran into some of his football game watching buddies one night, and they were looking at us with a not-so-sure what to say on their faces. It wouldn't be much longer before that little tidbit would reach Diana's ears, and we were right.

Diana stormed into Aaron's office a few days later, demanding to know what was going on between us. She had been told by someone she wished not to say, we were out having dinner together one night. I could hear her yelling at Aaron, and her calling me a scrawny alley cat all the way to my room. Aaron played it off smoothly telling her I had made a huge milestone in my recovery, and he took me out to celebrate. She ranted about how much longer was he going to support the low life that was doing nothing but mooching off him, and his generosity. Aaron continued telling her it was none of her business what he was doing when Carrie Ann wasn't in his care at the house. He wasn't yelling at her for all the men she has dated before, and after their divorce, so she shouldn't have any reason to be yelling at him for having dinner out with me.

That must have shut her up as she flew through the kitchen and out the back door slamming it shut in the process behind her. I heard her start her car, and stones hit the house as she drove off. She was definitely mad for sure. I wasn't sure if I should go see Aaron or not, but I did.

When I went to Aaron's office he was on the phone with his attorney telling him what had happened, warning him that he'll probably hear from her attorney within the next few days. He was just getting Eric ready for the tantrums by Diana.

It didn't stop Aaron from smiling, and motioning me to come in when he saw me. He was off that call, clasped his hands together rubbing them back and forth. He wasn't upset with the showdown he had just had with Diana. He was standing his ground with her more and more lately, and he was actually enjoying it. Before, he would just bow down to her whim, but not anymore. I was glad to see that.

I told him I heard everything from my room. I didn't want to be the cause of problems with Diana, and offered to find a place of my own, but Aaron's face lit up, saying no way should I be moving out . This was his house, and he could have whom ever he wants there. With that, he came over to hold me in his arms telling me not to worry, he was the one in control of his life finally, and Diana wasn't going to tell him how to live it any longer.

CHAPTER 11

Aaron knew Diana pretty well, because it wasn't long before Eric came by to tell him just that. Diana was going to stop Aaron from having Carrie Ann all summer next year, as long as I was living in the same house. She felt it wasn't healthy for Carrie Ann to see us together, and do what ever she thinks we're doing.

Aaron had until May to decide what he wanted to do about it, and with that Eric left. Aaron knew what he wanted to do, and had planned it out since my accident. He wouldn't elaborate what it was, but he was certain I would agree.

That weekend he didn't have Carrie Ann, which was no surprise to him seeing that she had made her demands known through Eric. She used the excuse she needed her at her house to help with her Christmas party. Her parties were mostly her friends she had met in the bars, and Aaron wasn't very happy to have Carrie Ann around all of them.

With that news, Aaron and I made plans for dinner for ourselves. I let Aaron decide where, and all he told me was that I needed to wear my black dress, and was gone for most of the morning. He didn't say where or why, but it gave me time to get my physical therapy done, and rest, which I knew I would need after that.

I took a long soak in the tub, and dressed in the black dress like he asked. I chose flat heeled shoes for now, seeing that I hadn't tried to walk in high heels since my accident.

When he came to my room to get me he smiled, and told me I was absolutely beautiful. I felt beautiful too, and being with him made everything perfect.

We arrived at the restaurant and was escorted to our table, by the huge windows looking out to the wooded area. The place was exquisite, and decorated for Christmas as well. The fireplace was burning logs that set off other colors other than the red, orange, and blue. There were poinsettias all over the room. It was absolutely breath taking.

After our delicious meal, Aaron ordered a bottle of champagne. It was poured into beautiful glasses, by the waiter. Once the waiter left, Aaron took my hand telling me how beautiful I was, how much he loved me, and how he can't imagine spending the rest of his life without me. I have healed his heart like he never thought would happen to him again.

As he moved off his chair, he got down on one knee holding a ring box opened exposing the most beautiful diamond ring I had ever seen. There was complete silence in the room from everyone else in there. As he spoke asking me if I would marry him, to be at his side for the rest of our lives, I could barely get out my answer, but shook my head in yes, as he slipped the ring on my finger.

I couldn't have been more surprised, or happier at that moment, and the other customers having dinner clapped, and smiled at us. I kissed Aaron right then knowing I would love him for always.

He made a toast with his glass of champagne as we drank what had been poured. It was the most beautiful moment of my life, and I felt as if my heart was going to burst through my chest with happiness.

We left the restaurant with me smiling from ear to ear. I was overjoyed with happiness. I couldn't wait to see his grandmother, and aunt to share what had just happened. Aaron called asking Molly and Mary to meet us at the house, while we drove back. When we arrived, they were talking at the counter in the kitchen. Both looked up as we walked in with curious looks on their faces.

As Aaron started to tell them what a great meal we had at Choppers, I blurted out that we were engaged, holding my left hand up flashing the engagement ring before them. Both women jumped from their stools, and hugged us both, as if they hadn't seen us in years. It was wonderful!

They congratulated us kissing our cheeks over and over. Molly had told me she was hoping Aaron would come to his senses making me his wife, but they also hadn't known his intent. That was something only Aaron had known, because he wanted it to be a complete surprise on his own accord.

Mary asked if we picked out a wedding date yet, and Aaron chuckled saying tomorrow, if he had his way. We all got a chuckle from that, but he was serious, dead serious. Aaron didn't want to wait another moment, and neither did I actually.

Molly asked if he could wait until next week, and do it at the family Christmas party where everyone could witness the wonderful occasion with us.

Aaron turned to me asking if that would be okay with me. We had talked on the way to the house that we both didn't want a huge wedding. I couldn't have thought of a better time, or a better place. Besides, the place was already decorated. It was perfect as far as we were concerned.

We went into Aaron's office and Mary brought in a pot of coffee and mugs, as we threw out all kinds of ideas of what we could do, and how we could pull it off without anyone knowing, or suspecting. Molly suggested that only the four of us should know any of the plans, and she was very serious when she spoke. She was worried that Diana would throw a wrench into everything, if she found out, or not allow Carrie Ann attend which would hurt both Aaron and Carrie Ann, down the road when she would find out.

We agreed, and continued with the plans late into the night. It was very exciting and yet, overwhelming at the same time. Aaron and I would go to the court house just before closing the Friday before, to get our license. The news wouldn't get out until after we were married, and Diana would be left in the dark.

I was letting Aaron decide where we would go for a honeymoon, but let him know I didn't need Hawaii, Paris, or the Bahamas. I would be happy just being with him in a quiet place not far away.

Once we had made all the plans, Molly and Mary hugged us both and left. It was already after midnight, but we had made great progress on the plans. All of which was feasible, to be done within a weeks time frame.

Molly, Mary, and I were going to the city in the morning to look for a wedding gown for me, and a new special dress for themselves as well. We were going to make a day of it shopping until we found exactly what we wanted, and have lunch at that little café we all liked so much. It was just so exciting making the plans with Aaron, Molly, and Mary.

Aaron and I made a few other plans before we walked to our bedrooms, but this time when he was kissing me goodnight I grabbed him by his shirt, and brought him in my room all the while kissing him. He definitely didn't expect that. He actually asked me if it was really what I wanted. I nodded yes, he dimmed the lights down, and scooped me into his arms kissing me. He gently laid me on my bed before lowering himself next to me. Our kisses were exploding by the time we made love that night.

By early morning we had made love a few more times. Our bodies couldn't get enough of each other, and the desire wouldn't release us until we were exhausted. We heard Mary open the backdoor, I scrambled to cover myself, as Aaron scooted into his bathroom to shower.

Once Aaron was done, I showered myself, and got ready to go shopping. Mary made us breakfast, which I gobbled down. Not only was I hungry, I was excited for the shopping to begin. Shopping for the most important day of my life, my wedding. It couldn't be better.

I kissed Aaron a good long kiss before Mary and I left, whispering he better rest because I planned on continuing where we left off this morning when I got back home. He chuckled telling me he'd be counting down the minutes.

We picked Molly up at her store, and was on our way to the city. More plans were made in the car, and they so were thoughtful thinking of what I wanted. After all, it was my wedding, not theirs, but they were grateful I wanted them to help me. Molly was the only one that had a daughter, and she had eloped, so they were happy take the opportunity to help me. I understood completely. Not having a mother of my own to help me, or be excited and happy for me, made it nice having them there to help.

I found the perfect gown I wanted with shoes that went together, as if they were made special to be with that gown. I didn't need a veil because I was going to just weave baby breath and miniature poinsettias in my hair that would match the small nosegay bouquet I planned to carry. Both Molly and Mary had tears in their eyes when I stepped out onto the platform in our assigned dressing room. They agreed with my choice.

I found a red party dress for Carrie Ann that would be so cute on her. She always had several different pairs of shoes, but the red Mary Jane shoes just went with the dress so well, that I purchased them also.

Mary was an ordained minister that would be officiating, as well as, baking the cake, with plenty of tiers and elaborations. I saw the cake topper I wanted before we checked completely out of that shop. We had a photographer already hired to take photos of the Christmas party that would be paid extra that night for our wedding, if needed.

Both Mary and Molly found gowns that they looked absolutely beautiful in, with shoes to match. We ate lunch at the little café and keeping our voices low we continued talking about everything. I couldn't wait knowing the next six days were going to feel like years to me.

Molly was the first to tell me that they were so happy

Aaron finally got around to asking me. They were so happy to have me be part of the family. Molly told me she just knew Aaron was in love with me after he started asking so many questions when I worked for her. Molly said she couldn't be anymore happier for us, and told me Aaron had finally told her he was in love with me when I was in the hospital. He had been so upset, but finally blurted it out that he might lose me, and he couldn't bare to think he would because he loved me so much.

I told her I thought I had heard them talking, but didn't know if I had been dreaming it, but now I knew it was no dream. As soon as Aaron was in the room after I had gotten cleaned up, he told me then how much he loved me. They both sighed saying how romantic at the same time, and chuckled. They both agreed it was about time!

That night after I was dropped off from shopping, Aaron was waiting for me. He swooped me into his arms kissing me so tenderly allowing the passion to build. We both knew where that was leading to, and that was where we went. I couldn't get enough of Aaron. My body ached for more until I was satisfied, and completely exhausted. We fell asleep with Aaron holding me in his arms. It felt good to be wanted by this man of mine, and I was going to make him the happiest man I could as his wife.

When Mary came the next morning, we sat at the counter while Aaron worked in his office. He had another book almost done, and the publisher was on him to finish it before the holidays. It gave me time to talk with Mary alone, and that was good. She didn't need to be there that day, but she had to do something before she went crazy at the house.

I asked her how bad was it when Diana was there,

and boy did she tell me things. Aaron never told me, but Diana did everything she could to make his life miserable. She was pregnant when they got married, and tried to convince everyone Carrie Ann was born premature, but an eight pound two ounce baby is not a premature baby. The doctor even told them it was full term. The deceit of that was only the beginning. Diana was rude to Molly and her wanting them away from Aaron, but yet she didn't want to do anything in the house, including care for Carrie Ann. It had been more important to go out with her friends night after night coming in so late, and too tired to care for her baby the next day.

Aaron never complained because she threatened to take Carrie Ann with her, and he would never see her again. Diana was what every store owner loved having in their store because she spent money as fast as she could on her whims.

Whenever Aaron tried to talk to her about her spending, she threw up the fact she could leave whenever he says, but he knew what that entailed…the loss of his daughter, and he couldn't bare the thought of that. Aaron put up with it until he walked in on her with another man in bed in his house. That was the last straw. Both Molly and Mary suspected that had been going on before, but until she spilled the beans, they weren't sure of it.

Aaron filed for divorce that afternoon while Diana made threats and demands. It was an ugly divorce, and when she didn't get everything she wanted, she threw a temper tantrum like a two year old right there in court in front of everyone.

Aaron had to pay her a hefty amount of alimony for

the next five years, or if she remarried before the five years was up, along with monthly child support other than the summer when Aaron would have her himself. He had no issue with the child support because he loved Carrie Ann, and he wanted everything for her.

Diana had asked Aaron for more money when she ran low. Almost lost her house because she over spent. Aaron gave her money just so Carrie Ann would have a place to live that was safe, and comfortable.

Mary ended with the warning that if Diana finds out about us getting married before we are married, she would most definitely cause problems. They would be ugly lies to make us look bad, and try to keep Aaron from Carrie Ann. I smiled and said, "let her bring it on," and Mary nodded saying, "good girl," as she patted my hand.

Diana may think she's in control of everything, but she was nothing more than a persnickety bitch as far as I was concerned.

CHAPTER 12

Our wedding day arrived and everything was in place to make it happen, and doing it all our way. Guests started arriving around six, and were having a great time mingling with each other. Diana dropped Carrie Ann off thinking she was going to stay for the party, but Aaron said it was for family only. She huffed as she turned making her way out the door. We dodged one problem there, and I was glad she didn't see me. She would have questioned why I could stay, and not her.

Aaron looked so handsome in his tuxedo as he walked around talking with the guests with the happiest look on his face. I had never seen him look so at ease with everything, as he did then. Once everyone that had been invited was there, and we had greeted them all, I slipped upstairs to where I had everything ready to change into my gown.

Molly helped Carrie Ann get into her new party dress,

and was as cute as a button. Aaron made his way to her room telling her he had something special to tell her that was going to happen tonight, and told her he was going to marry me. I heard her squeal with happiness down the hall. Aaron was glad she was happy, and accepted it as easily as she did. He knew Carrie Ann loved me as much as I love her, but the thought that I would be a part of the family was what Aaron was worried about. I would be a permanent fixture at the house, and sometimes the kids resent having a step-mom. I vowed I was going to do everything possible not to let that happen.

Aaron and I talked several times throughout the week on his concerns how Carrie Ann would act, but he had nothing to worry about. Carrie Ann told him she had asked Santa last year for this very thing. That was something we were both surprised over.

He returned downstairs patently waiting for me to come down the stairs to him. We were going to walk to his aunt together. I didn't have anyone to walk me to him so we decided we would walk together. He had his one foot on the bottom step making small talk with his cousins, while keeping his eyes on where I would be coming from. I could see him through the crack in the door as my heart was racing. I was so full of love for Aaron and couldn't be any more happier.

Once Carrie Ann walked down the stairs carrying a basket of red and white poinsettias, it was time for me. I began to slowly move as nervous as I was, while I watched Aaron's face light up when he saw me. He patted his heart with his hand, and smiled. I was ready to burst into tears just seeing the look on his face. I carefully made my way down the steps, hoping my legs wouldn't give out on me. When Aaron took my hand, I noticed his eyes were full of tears himself. Happy tears about to fall. I wiped them away with the tissue in my hand that I was using for myself.

He pulled me into his arms telling me I was absolutely the most beautiful woman ever, and how much he loved me. With the smile on his face, he said we need to get this going now, because he couldn't wait any longer to make me his wife. Leave it to Carrie Ann, she started towards the living room where Mary was waiting for us by the stone fireplace. The harpist started playing the traditional "Here Comes the Bride" and Carrie Ann was announcing, "make room for the bride and groom."

Our guests looked at us surely surprised as they opened a path for us to go through to reach Mary. Mary was standing in front of the fireplace at the end of the room with tears flowing like a river ready to hear our vows, and exchange rings so she could pronounce us husband and wife.

Aaron and I both said our own vows for the service pledging our lives to making the other always happy, and to love each other until death, and even beyond. Our exchange of gold bands finished the service, and Mary pronounced us husband and wife.

Aaron cupped my face bringing his mouth to mine in the longest sweetest kiss ever, and when he released me he smiled saying I made him the happiest man alive that night. Also, that he had meant every word he said in his vows to me. I giggled bringing his lips back to mine, and I kissed him as well.

Everyone clapped, and when I turned I don't think there was a dry eye in the room. Molly was right there passing out tissue to everyone, wiping her eyes as well. I didn't care then, I was so happy I let my own tears fall.

After all the congratulations, hugs, and kisses, we had a full course meal before cutting the cake. Everyone had a great time celebrating with us. Both Molly and Mary gave a toast to us as everyone lifted their champagne filled glasses in agreement. It couldn't have been planned any better than what we had done, and in such a short amount of time.

The photographer snapped his camera so often I started seeing spots every where I looked. Aaron held on to my hand the entire night planting kisses on me whenever he could. No one wanted to leave, but knew it was late. Besides, we had to get on with our honeymoon.

I stood on the third step of the staircase as I turned to toss my bouquet of miniature red poinsettias and baby breath, to the single women waiting below. Aaron tossed my garter, after he carefully took it off my leg with all the jokes he had to endure as he did so.

As we made our way down the front steps to the car, we were showered with rice. Carrie Ann was staying with Molly and Mary for the next few days. As we started to drive away, she ran over to kiss her daddy, and gave me one as well, telling us she loved us both, and that she was so happy.

Such a sweet ending to our special day. I was in seventh heaven as we waved to everyone and drove away.... destination unknown.

Aaron drove to their lake house in the country. It was a spectacular place with floor to ceiling windows overlooking the lake. The lights were on outside giving way to a wonderful sight that was hard to describe other than breath taking.

Aaron scooped me up into his arms as he carried me over the threshold straight to the bedroom.

As we were laying down I took his face into my hands, and told him I meant every word I said during our vows as they are that important to me. And I knew, I would always love him for the rest of our lives. My whole being was for him, and with him always.

$\mathcal{E}$PILOGUE

S everal years down the road, and after our honeymoon at the lake house, we spent many summers there that I know Aaron enjoyed as much as I did. When Aaron said he hadn't been there in such a long time without saying why, I knew. He and Carrie Ann were the only ones who spent time there. He didn't have to tell me Diana loathed it. Sometimes he would escape the house to do his writing here, where it was peaceful and calming, and I certainly could understand why.

I could see why he liked it so much. What was there not to like? Everything needed was there. No busy street with the traffic noise, no people around all the time, so many things to do, it made it a perfect get away.

In the afternoons, we'd take a walk on the trail around the lake. It really wasn't as large as I thought it was the night I first saw the place, but it was still wonderful. Aaron and I saw deer eating under the pine trees many times with plenty of birds that chirped as we walked. I brought my camera and snapped photos of everything, and plenty of Aaron happy in his element every time.

Our five kids enjoyed it there with all the adventures in the wooded areas as well as the water activities on the lake. Carrie Ann joined us every summer, and all six kids made plenty of memories with us. I couldn't have asked for anything better in our lives.

I finished my degree at college shortly after we were married opening a book store in the same plaza as Molly's boutique, with the large settlement I received from Miss Nelson's lawsuit. It may have taken awhile to finally sign off on the lawsuit, but it was well worth the wait.

I stocked all of Aaron's books, along with a large variety of other books, and genres. Our son, Andrew, followed his father's foot steps by becoming an author himself, but in the genre of children's literature. He was very successful, which made us both very proud.

I devoted one entire section of my book store for the history of the town, and its founders, the Malone family, of Jasper. Also an area others could work on their own genealogy of their family, with my help. It was busy non-stop from the minute the door was unlocked until closing.

Alex and Annabel Grace became attorneys opening a firm together in the same building Aaron's grandfather ran his legal affairs out of, which was also very successful.

Anson and Adam both became realtors, as well as flippers of homes. They had their own television program doing the homes exclusively in Jasper. That business kept them very busy, and it helped the community stay strong and beautiful.

Carrie Ann became a interior designer working along side of Anson and Alex when staging the homes to be sold. She was very good at it making more money than what she ever thought she would.

Jonathan and Amber's house, as well as Miss Nelson's house, were purchased by Anson and Alex for themselves. They had Carrie Ann decorate the homes and she did an amazing job. Carrie Ann moved into the apartment above our garage until she married. She then moved into Molly and Mary's home after they passed away.

All five of our kids chose wonderful spouses and started having their own children shortly. The Malone family was growing by leaps and bounds. It was wonderful.

We continue to have our Malone traditions every year, and in memory of Aaron, we still meet at the lake house several times in the summer to reminisce, and enjoy everything that had meant so much to Aaron, his aunt Mary, and grandmother, Molly.

Diana had a life that wasn't as good, but she was the one who treated Aaron so poorly. I was the one who reaped her poor choices. She has married and divorced three more times before she decided to stay single, and finally living in an assisted living facility. She had tried several times to get back in grace with Aaron, and he told her she had her chance and blew it. He was happy now, and nothing was going to change that.

Carrie Ann came to live with us when she turned twelve by going through the court system. Diana only wanted in her life when she needed money, which Carrie Ann would only give her a little allowance weekly. Diana didn't have any other children after Carrie Ann by choice, which I feel sorry for her on that. The joy our kids have brought us is priceless, and she would never have the wonderful feelings and memories as we do.

Aaron was, and always would be, the best thing that happened in my life, and as I held his hand telling him I love him with all my being. He smiled telling me he loved me touching his heart as he did from the beginning of our life together, and closed his eyes for the final time.

I miss him tremendously every second of the day, but our children have kept me busy with the families they now have, and I know the love is always there for us. Aaron would be so pleased with everything.

About the Author

Joann Buie

Joann was born and raised in Ashtabula, Ohio, and liked writing short stories and numerous poems for others to read. Two hours after graduating from high school, she moved to Michigan to be with her husband, Bo, who was serving in the Air Force.

Moving to Arizona in 1979 as a young mother of three, Joann went to work in the school district in the Special Education department while completing her Bachelor's Degree. She earned her Master's Degree from Northern Arizona University while teaching elementary education.

After over twenty years working in the educational field and living over forty years in Arizona, she retired and now resides in Florida with her husband and two little dogs, Charlie Brown and Lucy.

Joann has been married for over fifty years, has three grown children and is a grandmother to seven.